SERIAL KILLER PRINCESS

A Magical Romantic Comedy (with a body count)

RJ BLAIN

Warning: This novel contains excessive humor, action, excitement, adventure, magic, romance, and bodies. Proceed with caution.

Why would anyone put a mermaid and a gorgon in the same room together? While Tulip enjoys being alive, her lineage brings her nothing but trouble.

Snakes eat fish, and the mer love tearing apart their serpentine nemeses with their hands and teeth. As for the gorgons… she'd rather not think about them at all.

The last thing Tulip wants is to rule the mer kingdom. First, she can barely swim. Second, she's packing more than her fair share of her father's genes. Third, what is a landlocked princess supposed to do with an aquatic kingdom?

If she gets her way, nothing. Add in her dirty little serial killing secret, and she's an international disaster waiting to happen.

There's just one small problem: her father's bodyguard tempts her in ways no one should, and if she isn't careful, he'll uncover her secrets, domesticate her, and infect her with a severe case of normality.

Cover design by Rebecca Frank of Bewitching Book Covers.

ONE

I could've done a better—and more
interesting—job with a rusty spoon.

WHAT THE HELL did a girl need to do to catch a break? I'd spent the worst six months of my entire fucking life hunting a limp dick with a complex so I could finally wring the life out of his wretched little body only to discover someone had gotten to him first. To add insult to injury, I could've done a better—and more interesting—job with a rusty spoon. Forget a rusty spoon, I could do things with a toothpick capable of making detectives weep.

Where was the art in a slit throat? Matthew Henders hadn't slit the throats of victims. He was the take them home, lock them in his basement, and rape them kind, and he didn't give a shit what species or gender his victims were. I would've done such a better job of murdering him, and I resented the piss poor albeit effective technique.

Who slit a serial killer's throat and left his body lying around for anyone to find? What ever happened to the artistry of a good premeditated murder?

I'd spent months planning his death, right down to the

day and time, exactly ten years to the minute after his first killing. I scowled at the body, which was sprawled on his front step, and heaved a sigh. Twice. One sigh simply wasn't sufficient. It had to be two. Three was a bit too dramatic, even for me.

Since finding his body on his doorstep wasn't part of my plan, I did the only sensible thing a woman posing as a mail courier could do. I screamed, I flailed, I flung his package up and over my head in the general direction of the street, and screamed some more. Instead of wasting half a year hunting an asshole serial killer, I should've gone to Hollywood and made some money screaming for pay.

I could teach sirens a thing or two about a good, shrill scream, and if those bitches tried to tell me otherwise, I'd break their teeth before taking my time finding an appropriately gruesome way to kill them. Sirens counted as serial killers. Sailors around the world would thank me for thinning their population.

And since my day wasn't sucking enough already, Matthew Henders's box exploded.

Why did I always get the mail bombs? Oh, right. I liked posing as a delivery girl when hunting serial killers. I really needed a new life—or a better gig. Instead of a mail courier, I'd switch to pizza. At least pizzas smelled good and didn't tend to blow up in my face.

As far as bombs went, I'd gotten a small one. I could deal with small ones. I could even deal with them while flat on my back on my target's sidewalk, little bright bubbles of light swirling prettily in front of my eyes, the shit stunned out of me. Fortunately for my dignity and pride, it wasn't literal shit.

There was an entire chapter in the Modern Guide to

Being a Princess handbook dedicated to the subject of bodily functions. Under no circumstances did a princess have the shit startled out of her. A feminine scream, even a piercing one, was permitted, but there was a solid ban against brown trousers time. The handbook's author also had opinions about princesses who had the piss scared out of them, too.

In a word, no.

I really hated that book. It sucked the joy out my life.

At least it didn't have anything in it banning lying prone on the ground in a dead man's blood. *My* blood was a different matter.

According to the Modern Guide to Being a Princess, princesses farted floral-scented rainbows, always found someone to bleed for them, and cared more about their nails than life itself. I had three words to say to the author of the book the next time I saw the bitch: fuck that shit.

Unfortunately for me, the bitch was my mother.

One day, I'd take my mother to task for her stupid idea of a joke. What sort of mermaid queen wrote a handbook for a land-locked princess? Her stupid little handbook, a mocking Christmas present meant to remind me she hadn't forgotten about me, had made the rounds, polluting the bookshelves of royal families around the world. I bet my father and his hive of gorgon ladies had a copy just to spite me. I'd never even met the man, not that I wanted to.

All of life's problems began and ended with mermaids and gorgons, and I did my best to avoid both sides of the fence.

Emergency sirens wailed in the distance. With the pretty lights still bubbling through my vision, something smoking nearby—probably my damned delivery truck—and a whopper of a headache, playing victim seemed like a good idea. I even liked ambulance rides. They amused the hell out of me, especially with a concussion, where I could get away with breaking even more of my mother's rules.

Princesses didn't whine, so I'd practice my best pout while I kept my eyes open long enough to make them water and blur. Princesses didn't cry, the one rule I agreed with, so while I'd play the dewy-eyed maiden in distress for shits and giggles, not a single damned one would fall. I'd totally angle for a lollipop from the triage nurse, though.

They laced the damned things with pixie dust, and riding on a cloud-nine high might dull the edge of my disgust over having been robbed of my kill. Who the hell wasted a serial killer's death slitting his throat? I needed to find the murderer and show him a thing or two about how to kill somebody.

While I waited for the ambulance, I considered getting up. Lying in a pool of blood wasn't exactly comfortable, especially since I had no idea what sort of nasty contagions my dead mark had contracted over the years. With my luck, he probably had lycanthropy, then the damned doctors would start poking me to find out if I'd contracted the infection. Telling the doctor to go back to medical school because neither gorgons nor mermaids could contract lycanthropy wouldn't do me any good. What looked like a human, walked like a human, and talked like a human was obviously human, and humans contracted lycanthropy.

Stupid doctors liked poking holes in my arguments. If I was a gorgon's whelp, why didn't I have snakes for hair? If I was a mermaid, why didn't I grow fins when I got wet?

Of course, the real idiot was me for not even bothering trying to get up, waiting with princess-perfect patience for my lovely ride in an ambulance so I could get a pixie dust lollipop. Where else was I going to get my damned lollipop?

Princesses did not, under any circumstance, resort to recreational drugs to turn a bad day around.

I really needed my damned lollipop. The instant my mother found out I was in the United States working as a mail courier again, she'd take her royal scepter and shove it up my ass. The first four or five times had been bad enough. I could already hear her questioning what sort of princess worked as a mail courier.

'The best kind' was not the answer she wanted.

One day I would learn. When I did, I would suggest my mother should add a chapter to her precious little handbook. It would be very short. It would instruct princesses there was nothing dumber in life than pissing off Queen Mother, AKA Megabitch Supreme.

I'd need two lollipops to get through the rest of my day, because there was no way in hell I was picking myself off the sidewalk and making my grand escape before the cops showed up. Considering the sirens blared at ear-throbbing volume, they'd already arrived. The slap of shoes on concrete confirmed my belief, and I squinted in my effort to make my eyes cooperate with me.

Two men in the dark blue uniforms of American police officers leaned over me. The old bald one, a black dude with more dark splotches on his cheeks than the average ladybug, looked rather concerned. The other one, a nice little chestnut number with wide blue eyes and the kind of tan I dreamed about having, looked like he needed me to rip him out of his uniform and show him a good time.

Fortunately for me, there was nothing in the Modern Guide to Being a Princess banning the admiration of a fine law enforcement officer. There were many rules about not touching them for some reason, though.

Stupid rules. I needed to burn that handbook the next time my mother gave me a copy, which I expected to be by tomorrow morning. In person.

Joyous day. Absolutely stupendous.

"I think the guy I was delivering a package to died and then his package blew up," I slurred.

Huh. Maybe the bomb had packed a bit more punch than I thought—or my head wasn't nearly as hard as my mother made it out to be. Either way, slurring was firmly in the 'not good' column. Then again, there were pretty lights still dancing around my vision, the pesky things. Ah, concussions. I gave it an hour before my brain tried to dribble out of my ears.

The hot cop frowned, stepped around me, and gave me a good look at his back. Nice. America truly did have some lovely scenery. He unhooked some doohickey from his vest and talked to someone on it before turning to face me. "An ambulance has been dispatched, ma'am."

I admired how he gave a statement and asked a question at the same time, subtle enough I could ignore his request for my name if I wanted. In all honesty, I wanted to do a legal name change, but if I did, my mother would hunt me down and make me wish she'd actually murder me.

All delaying would do was prolong my suffering. The sooner I said it, the sooner they'd quit laughing. "Tulip Flandersmythe."

My mother needed to explain why she'd named me after a bunch of flowers. Tulip was bad enough, but if anyone found out my middle names were Daisy Lilac Petunia, I'd never live it down. Why *had* she given me three middle names, anyway? I bet it was because she hated me from the moment of my birth and wanted me to know it. Then, because expressing eternal hatred wasn't sufficient, she insisted on doting on me whenever absolutely possible. If she couldn't get rid of me through giving me the worst name on the planet, she'd love me to death.

My queen mother needed her scepter shoved up her ass for inflicting such a horrible name on me. I was no wilting lily. I killed serial killers because I could, and I got away with it because I was good at it.

Killing people was *definitely* not allowed according to the Modern Guide to Being a Princess. Absolutely not allowed. Princesses had servants and bodyguards for that.

The old cop's eyes widened, a huffy little snort bursting out of him.

"Go ahead and laugh. Wouldn't want to give you a stroke or something. The rest of my name's even worse."

"I'm not sure how that's even possible," Mr. Dreamy muttered and crouched beside me, careful to keep his shiny shoes out of Matthew Henders's blood. He held up a single finger. "Miss Flandersmythe, can you please tell me how many fingers I'm holding up?"

I showed him my middle finger, a rather accurate portrayal of what I thought of his tone. "I'm aware I hit my head, you're holding up one finger, yes, my vision is blurry, I realize I'm slurring, and even a dainty mail carrier like me can identify a concussion. Really. Also, my mail blew up, and I'm lying in some dead guy's blood."

Ignoring my rude gesture, Mr. Dreamy grabbed hold of my arm and pressed his fingertips to my wrist, his gaze shifting away from me to his watch. With a frown, he released my hand, leaned forward, and touched my throat.

Not only was he handsome, he was hot, too—uncomfortably so. I sighed.

Of course, I suffered from shock. I just couldn't catch a break, could I? Then again, I hadn't actually broken anything. Concussions and shock I could deal with. Broken bones sucked. Shock was a step up from breaking something. Resigned to the inevitable, I moved my arm enough to dig out my wallet from my pocket and offered it to the cop. "ID and health insurance card are in front lower slot."

Mr. Dreamy took my wallet, opened it, and pulled out the two cards. "Thank you. This'll simplify things. While we wait for the ambulance to arrive, why don't you tell me about your day?"

I did, although I left out the part about having come to Matthew Henders's house to kill him. That would put a damper on our relationship.

INSTEAD OF A LOLLIPOP, I got an MRI and a hard time from a cute doctor. He wasn't quite up to the standards of Mr. Dreamy, but he put up a good fight. I wanted a damned lollipop, he refused to give me one, and apparently since he was a damned doctor, he won by default.

"What do you have against lollipops?" I complained, swinging my legs while sitting on the examination table. "Come on, doc. Just one."

"Only good patients or children get lollipops, and you are neither." The doc stared at his clipboard, clicking his pen.

"What's got your panties in a bunch, doc? Is my brain going to take a hike?"

"Your skull isn't cracked and swelling appears minimal, but there's minor bleeding." The doc approached me and touched my neck near the base of my skull. "Here. I suspect it happened when you fell. I doubt there's reason for concern, but observation for the next twenty-four hours is mandatory. I'll have another MRI done in twelve hours to confirm your condition. While your slurring has improved, it's a potential cause for concern."

Why did American hospitals take so many unnecessary precautions? While I scowled, I waved my hand in acceptance of his decree. "Fine. Twenty-four hours. I think it's unnecessary, but you're the doc."

"There's just an issue of your room assignment."

"Whoever is stuck with me should probably get two lollipops."

"So you can steal one?"

"Exactly."

"That's fortunate, since this hospital doesn't have private rooms." The doc slipped a sheet of paper from the bottom of his stack and waved it around in my face. "Nor do we use titles."

If I pretended the problem of my birth didn't exist, maybe no one would attempt to saddle me with a title. Who needed a damned title, anyway? Not me. I averted my gaze, lifted my chin, and gave a dainty sniff. "What title?"

"Your Highness," a man's pleasant tenor announced from the door. I recognized the voice, and despite the pounding in my head, I comprehended two things at once.

Wherever Terrance the Grumpy went, my mother was never far behind. By not far behind, she was usually within twenty feet, which gave me less than a minute to jump out the nearest window. I scrambled off the examination table and darted for freedom, making it four whole steps before my mother's bodyguard clotheslined me.

For a merman at least five times my age, the bastard packed a punch. Instead of smacking into the floor like I deserved, my back slammed into his chest. Terrance even managed to pin both my elbows to my side with one arm. "Have I told you how much you suck, Terrance?"

"My life wouldn't be complete without being graced with the showering of your affections, Your Highness."

"You don't have to sound so grumpy about it." Actually, Terrance sounded far more amused than grumpy, and I wasn't sure what I thought about that.

"Do be careful with my patient, sir. If you'd like to restrain her, please do so on the examination table."

Instead of letting me walk like the capable woman I was, Terrance tightened his hold on me, straightened, and carried me to the table as though I weighed nothing. He released me long enough to set his hands on my waist, lift me up, and set me exactly where I'd been when he'd entered the room. To add insult to injury, he patted me on the head like he'd done since I'd been old enough to walk.

Death was too good of a fate for Terrance the Grumpy. "Terrance," I grumbled.

"Yes, Your Highness?"

I pointed at the cute doctor. "No titles are permitted at this hospital."

"There'll also be no bodyguards terrorizing my patients," my doctor helpfully contributed.

Despite his refusal to give me a lollipop, I decided I liked the American. "You should listen to him, Terrance." Preparing myself for the inevitable, I shot a glare at the door. "Is she here?"

"No, Your—"

Shifting my glare back to the head of my mother's security, I crossed my arms over my chest, the hospital gown rustling, proving it wasn't actually made of fabric despite its best efforts to disguise itself. "What do you mean she isn't here?"

"Her Royal Majesty is at home discussing with His Royal Majesty about securing a less troublesome replacement."

Okay, I had missed a very important memo. "His Royal Majesty?"

It drove the entire mer kingdom to utter distraction my mother didn't have a His Royal Majesty.

"Your father, of course. Much to the eternal disappointment of princes around the world, I'm sure." Terrance dipped a bow to me, smirked, and turned to the doctor. "My apologies, sir. I'm Terrance Marianas. Her Royal Majesty sent me to deal with any matters regarding her daughter." With a flick of his wrist, Terrance produced a small envelope sealed with the Flandersmythe royal seal, an albatross battling an osprey.

Most in the family favored the osprey for its tendency to crack open bones to get to the tasty marrow within, where I much preferred the albatross for its ability to fly without tiring. Then again, I was probably the only one in my family who longed to grow wings and fly.

Instead, I donned scales and slithered, not that my queen mother—or anyone—knew my little secret. There was an entire ten-page chapter in the Modern Guide to Being a Princess discussing why members of a royal family didn't indulge in weird magic. Destructive magic was one thing. A princess was encouraged to destroy invading armies with a sweep of her perfect, manicured hand.

Transforming into a serpent crossed a line, similar to the one firmly wedged between shrieking and pants pissing.

"Dr. Hausten." The doctor took the note, cracked the seal, and clucked his tongue a few times. "Very well, Mr. Marianas. These arrangements can be made. I can give you this room in the meantime. I'll ask one of the nurses to see to Miss Flandersmythe's clothing. While I'm afraid they're stained, they'll be clean."

Oh, nice. I marked the Minnesota hospital as my favorite of the American hospitals I'd been to. None of the other ones had bothered trying to clean the blood out of my clothes.

"Just give her a lollipop," Terrance replied, a smile ghosting across his lips. "That should keep her occupied for at least ten minutes. Should the lollipop be, ah, tainted per the American way, accidents do happen. I'm a very understanding gentleman."

Terrance? Understanding? A gentleman?

The head of my mother's security had been the first to show me how men died, although it'd been an accidental lesson thanks to the scheming of a greedy human hoping to capitalize on my existence. As my mother's sole child, she wasn't the only one who saw some odd value to my life.

Damned royal blood, always complicating matters for me.

"Didn't your mother tell you it's rude to lie, Terrance?" I smacked my palms to the paper-covered examination table and drummed my fingers. "Apparently, the doc here only gives lollipops to good patients and children."

"Of which you're neither. I suppose you'll just have to suffer without your American lollipop."

"Heartless, that's what you are."

Dr. Hausten didn't seem amused. "Should I be concerned about addiction, Mr. Marianas?"

My mother's head of security frowned, glancing in the doctor's direction. "Oh, no. Of course not. Pixies don't live where we're from, so Her Highness finds their dust and America's reliance on it fascinating, doctor."

"I see."

"I apologize for the inconvenience, but until the investigation is completed, I insist either myself or someone from my team remain with Her Highness."

My day went from bad to worse. While I longed to indulge in several good sighs, I kept quiet. All sighing would do was ensure Grumpy Head of Security stuck around even longer. At least I wouldn't have to try to hide a murder. Hiding a murder with Terrance around ranked as my least favorite activity ever.

Was there anything worse than mermen, always getting underfoot and making nuisances of themselves? No wonder my mother hadn't married despite having fulfilled her obligations to my father. I frowned, and comprehension struck me like a hammer right between the eyes. "Terrance? Did you say my mother was talking to my *father*?"

Since when did my parents speak? I didn't even know my father's name. My mother refused to talk about him, so I'd always assumed he was a rat bastard—or, well, a gorgon.

I'd never actually met a gorgon before.

Terrance checked his watch. "Indeed. The last I heard, she had offered him an American dollar if he'd take you off her hands. I think he's in progress of paying for you. When I was evicted and ordered to come to America, she'd moved on to negotiating for a replacement heir, one who won't continually insist on giving her gray hairs."

While my mother, Her Most Royal Majesty, had threatened to sell me to a circus a few times, I hadn't believed she'd actually do it. "Seriously? One dollar? That's it?"

"Her starting offer was a penny."

Maybe my name was Tulip Daisy Lilac Petunia Flandersmythe, but even I had *some* pride. Okay, I had a lot of pride, and I teetered on the edge of murderous fury and despair. "A penny!"

"She also thanks you for investing in your own medical insurance so she won't have to pay even more for you," Terrance the Grumpy announced.

The first thing I'd do the instant I got out of the hospital would be to find a copy of the Modern Guide to Being a Princess and burn the damned thing. In the next ten minutes, I planned on breaking every rule in the fucking handbook, and I'd start on page one. A princess didn't run from her security or put her life at risk. Making a break for the door at a sprint counted, especially since the slap of my bare feet on the shiny white tiles drove spikes through my head.

I ran for the hills.

I really couldn't catch a break, could I?

I COLLIDED with Mr. Dreamy halfway down the hallway, my breath leaving me in a rush. Whether by design or accident, we went down in a heap, and he took the brunt of our fall. The clap of Terrance's shoes on the floor promised hell in about ten seconds.

Damn it, I really couldn't catch a break, could I?

Since I was out to trash every rule in the book anyway, I did the first thing I could think of guaranteed to buy me a few seconds. I smacked both my hands to Mr. Dreamy's cheeks, planted a kiss on his lips using just enough tongue to make it indecent, and launched off him to implement the next phase of my escape.

American cops had nice mouths. He had big hands, too, which landed right on my ass in his attempt to catch me so I couldn't continue my mad dash for freedom. I wouldn't begrudge him copping a feel, and I'd send the hospital a note later thanking them for their slippery hospital gowns, as I slid right through his fingers.

"Princess Tulip!" Terrance barked.

"Princess?"

I wanted to enjoy Mr. Dreamy's stunned expression, which was surely a match for his tone, but a smart princess didn't make an opportunity and waste it admiring the fine American scenery. Bolting down the hall, I rounded the first corner, dodged a gurney, and beelined straight for a closing elevator, sliding through the gap in the doors and pressing the up and down buttons so I'd be able to continue my mad dash no matter which way the damned thing went.

The elevator's occupants gaped at me.

"Nothing to see here," I chirped, flashing my best smile.

The elevator went up a floor, dinged, and swooshed open. I took off at a jog, following the signs for the nearest stairwell. If my head was going to hurt anyway, I'd give it a reason to pound as I dove down the steps two or three at a time and practiced my rail-sliding skills. Rail sliding made escaping down convenient stairwells so much easier.

I'd be pissed if the hospital lacked good rails in their staircases.

I burst through the door, huffed my satisfaction at the lovely inner rail, and took a ride down to the next landing, bounced off the wall, and plunged down the staircase towards freedom.

A good serial killer with a preference for other serial killers always found a way out of a bad situation. Who needed a floor plan? The instant I found an emergency exit, I'd be a free woman. Of course, Terrance wouldn't quit until he found me, trussed me up, and carted me off wherever he wanted me to go. It'd be great fun for one of us. If I lasted a week, I'd call myself the victor.

The last time I'd given him the slip, I'd gotten away with

it for a record two days. Usually, he pinned me down within half an hour. Actually, I considered it an accomplishment I'd made it to the stairwell.

Terrance made a good adversary despite being just like every other merman on the planet, loyal to a fault, vicious only towards their dinner and threats, and uninterested in anything other than his duty to Her Royal Majesty. Once every few decades, the entire species took leave of its senses and headed for shore to mass reproduce, resulting in three years of mermaids and mermen eagerly awaiting the hatching of the next generation.

Only the insane approached a mer colony waiting for a hatching.

Maybe once I gave Terrance the slip, I'd sit down with my mother and have a talk with her. Instead of spawning a proper heir with a merman prince, Her Royal Majesty had picked a gorgon, spent ten months on shore to have me, and came to the disturbing discovery I'd be stuck on land for the rest of my life, resulting in her conquering a small island so I'd have somewhere to live within the heart of her kingdom. If love could be rated by one's willingness to conquer land-masses, my mother adored me. Personally, I thought she just liked conquering small islands, as she'd bequeathed me with three of the damned things, one off the coast of Europe, one near Africa, and one skirting China's southernmost shores.

I slid my way to the lowest floor only to discover I wasn't alone. Instead of bouncing off the wall as I'd done the other eight stories, I smacked face first into a man's chest. Damn it, I really needed to stop running into men, especially since my latest victim was about as hard as a rock. This time, however, I hit the floor without the benefit of someone breaking my fall.

My victim had really shiny shoes, one of which was an inch from my face.

"Nice oxfords," I mumbled.

"Thank you."

I sighed and got to my hands and knees. "If you could pretend this never happened, that'd be great."

"If you're trying to get out of the hospital, you'll be disappointed to learn the ways out are guarded to prevent a certain patient from escaping."

How nice. I'd collided with someone helpful, telling me things I already knew. "That does make things more entertaining."

"They even have alarms when patients run for it, alarms which have already been triggered. That's going to ruin your plan, I'm sorry to say."

Maybe I should have stayed with Mr. Dreamy, assaulting him for a bit longer. I could've gone for historically indecent rather than just mildly indecent. Terrance would've captured me right away, but at least I would've been able to enjoy a few more moments of a hot American's mouth. Instead, I got Mr. Shiny Shoes, who had a fetish for stating the obvious. "How nice."

It took me three tries to get to my feet, and when I did, I came nose to scale with a dozen or so black mambas. I recognized the damned things for one reason alone: I had a mirror and knew how to use it.

My good look into their black-lined mouths helped with their identification, too.

It was one thing to admire my scaly self in my reflection and another to have a bunch of them hissing in my face. I launched halfway into orbit with a shriek, landed on the bottom step, and bailed, scrambling for the first-floor landing. I hit the door at full throttle, plowed over someone in a white doctor's coat, and ran down the hallway, ducking into the first empty room I found, slamming the door behind me.

A crammed utility closet made the ultimate location to hide. I didn't bother stripping. I hit my knees, muttered a few curses, and broke several of my mother's precious little rules in one fell swoop, embracing my scaly side with a preference for warm, sunny places and enough venom to kill a horse.

The first time I'd shifted, I'd been alone on my island, thirteen, bored out of my mind, and contemplating swimming for the coast fifty miles away. The desire to go anywhere and be anyone else had triggered it, I supposed, and I'd spent the three days waiting for the vacationing staff to return poking my scaly nose places it didn't belong.

A mirror and the terror of being declared a freak had shunted me back to my human form, and a good thing, too. Mers hated snakes. I still wasn't sure how I'd been born in the first place. The last time a sea serpent had been foolish enough to cross Her Royal Majesty, it'd been torn to teeny tiny bits as an example—with her bare hands.

Then again, the damned thing had just bitten five-year-old me in the foot, landing me in the hospital for the first time in my memory. If I had come from a normal family, I would've used it, along with the conquering of several islands, as evidence my mother actually loved me.

The shifting process didn't take very long, giving me plenty of time to slither out of my crappy little hospital gown. I snagged it in my fangs and dragged it beneath one of the metal cabinets, my scales rasping on the tiles. It took me longer than I liked to stuff the damned thing behind a bucket, poking it into place with my nose. With a bit of fuss-ing, I could probably turn it into a rather cozy nest for myself.

The only problem with my plan was my lack of a plan. A face full of black mambas meant one thing alone: Mr. Shiny Shoes was a gorgon, not that I'd gotten a look at his face around his snakes. What other species had a bunch of snakes attached to their heads and wore shoes? I couldn't think of one.

Maybe my mother really had sold me to a gorgon for a dollar. Would a gorgon put in a whole lot of effort to find me if I bailed? Considering I knew absolutely nothing about my father, I—

Oh shit.

Most gorgons had harmless serpents for hair. I'd figured that much out when I'd gotten bored and checked on the internet. The more dangerous a gorgon's snakes, the higher up the totem pole they were, and black mambas were as close to the top as it got. There were more venomous snakes in the world, and a lot of them, but the more venomous ones couldn't deliver their toxins with the ready ease of a black mamba.

How many gorgons with black mambas existed in the world? Unfortunately, I had no idea and no way to find out. I did, however, understand one important thing. Under normal circumstances, gorgons didn't just show up at places like a hospital, not without a reason. There was only one gorgon I could think of who might even consider taking the necessary precautions to go out in public, and he'd purchased me from my mother for one whole dollar.

I slithered every inch of my fourteen slender feet into the corner behind the bucket, coiling so I took up as little space as possible. At least I did being a black mamba well; I probably broke records with my length, dwarfing the natural ones by six feet.

If I ran with the assumption gorgons with black mambas for hair came few and far between, my father had nice, shiny shoes.

For once in my life, I did exactly what the Modern Guide to Being a Princess suggested. When shit hit the fan, a wise princess found a place to hide until it was safe to come out.

IT DIDN'T TAKE LONG for someone to check the utility closet. The first time, they turned on the light, sighed, turned it back off, and left, closing the door behind them. The second time, they turned the light on, left it on, and the tap of something on the floor betrayed their plan to record any activity in the closet.

To everyone who thought they knew me, patience wasn't a virtue I possessed.

Those same people had no idea about my side job and the lengths I'd go to ensure the brutal death of a serial killer. Most of the time, I did it on the house, finding pleasure in the hunt while ensuring the safety of those my prey would've victimized. Every now and then, I picked up a legitimate bounty, gave myself a new call name, and demanded payment in the form of disposable credit cards. A few hours and several Swiss bank accounts later, the money disappeared, which I did just to fuck with Interpol, the FBI, and other crime fighting organizations who wanted a piece of me. There were a few, which never failed to amuse me.

I had no problem with coiling up and waiting for someone to come fetch their recording device, eager to savor their disappointment. My moment came much later, after a satisfying nap. Terrance didn't curse often, and I enjoyed every one he muttered. Footsteps entered the room, and from my hiding spot, I caught a glimpse of someone bending down to retrieve the device on the floor.

Patience was a virtue, but assumptions led me straight into trouble. It took a lot of effort to slither without my scales rasping, involving the slowest movements I'd ever made in my life. I wanted to hiss my agitation, but I remained silent, peeking under the cabinet.

Terrance had left me a new present, a camera most called a fish eye for its round shape and ability to record in all directions. Judging from its golf ball size, it was a fairly basic model, likely lacking motion detection. I glared at it.

It stayed still on the floor, as cameras tended to do when left unattended. In the staring contest department, it won without question, and I resented that enough I contemplated slithering out of my shadowy spot and eating the damned thing to teach it a lesson.

Since choking to death wasn't on my list of things to do, I waited, kept still, and watched the camera. Unlike watching paint dry, which *did* have visual changes over time, the camera did exactly nothing. Who was, if anyone, watching the recording? Did I care? If I didn't eat it, could I cover up the hospital gown and drag it into the corner with me?

I liked the idea, so I retreated, gathered the discarded gown, and used it to hide my beautiful, sleek gray body from the camera. It took time to bunch the thin material in front of me, but once set, within a minute, I nosed the fabric across the floor, covered the device, and looked for a way out of the room.

Even closets had ventilation ducts, and I spotted a rather

nice one with slits in the ceiling, plenty spacious for a slender beauty such as a myself to slip through. Coiling my tail around the gown and the camera, I dragged my prize along while I began the climb up the shelving unit.

I truly loved being a snake sometimes. With fourteen feet of muscle to work with, it didn't take long for me to jam my head into the vent. Luckily for me, the filter rested on a frame, making it easy to nose it aside so I could access the ducts. Slithering inside, I dragged the camera and gown behind me. With the camera trapped in the gown, it wouldn't fit through the gap. Displeased at the inconvenience, I pulled and jerked until the gown tore.

The fish eye camera crashed to the floor and shattered. The shredded ruins of the gown came with me, and I tugged it inside until none of it stuck out of the vent. Pleased with my work, I explored the hospital. Curiously, the ducts opened to second and third floors, pumping cool air into a wide assortment of places, even operating rooms. Many of the rooms had vents near the wall too narrow for me to slither through without having to dislodge the entire cover. The ones leading to the second floor offered the easiest ways to escape, as only a filter and the vent slit blocked my way to freedom.

I just needed to pick the perfect room to stage my escape.

I picked the kitchen, as it had food, it was warm, and it had several ways out. Why the kitchen was on the second floor was beyond me, but rather than questioning the architects, I watched and waited, flicking my tongue out to taste the air.

Someone below cooked meat, and I wanted to dine on it. I'd take it raw, seared, or even charred, but I wanted the meat. I poked my nose through the vent and observed the cooks below. After a few minutes, I determined half the kitchen cooked some form of beef stew while the other half made something with chicken and a lot of vegetables.

In a corner, isolated from the rest of the staff, was a pair of poor sobs making salad. I felt sorry for the people expected to eat the stuff. While I'd eat salad now and then, I had standards. Wilting lettuce, tomatoes that had been ripe a week ago, and almost respectable carrots classified as cruel and unusual punishment. Add in the white, plain dressing masquerading as ranch, and I pitied the patients.

After what felt like an eternity, the staff ferried out the prepared meals, bustling out of the kitchen. In a disgraceful show of waste, they left uncooked meat on the counters, ranging from chunks of stewing beef to raw chicken. I expected someone would come and dispose of it, but I thought they'd at least *try* to use everything.

A second and third check confirmed the kitchen was abandoned, and I slid out of the vent, angling in the direction of the counter and its pile of delicious red, raw meat. I couldn't quite reach, so I thumped to the floor, slithered my way to my dinner, and rose up, snatching chunks and swallowing them as fast as I could. I cleaned the cutting board, and still hungry, I crossed the kitchen and stole the chicken, too.

My bulging stomach would make navigating small places difficult, and I cursed myself for my weakness.

On the job, I took a lot of care with what I ate. However amusing, a toxic or noisy fart could sink me, and nothing was worse than having to take a piss during a stake out or while committing a good murder. In about an hour, I'd want to sleep off my dinner, which meant finding a new place to hide or getting out of the building as soon as possible.

Exploring the kitchen, I discovered a supply cart pushed off to the side, filled with plastic tubs meant to be reused. A quick inspection of the wheels and undercarriage revealed plenty of metal braces supporting the frame with gaps large enough for me to squeeze through. As long as no one looked beneath it and spotted my bulging tummy, I'd be free in no time at all.

THREE

I only killed people who deserved it.

THE HOSPITAL NEEDED to monitor their kitchen staff better. My patience only went so far, and by the time someone returned to the kitchen to begin the cleanup work, I wanted to bite people for their tardiness and lack of care.

No one noticed my theft of the leftover meat. Five people worked to restore the kitchen to rights, and I watched them from my place beneath the cart, the tip of my tail twitching. While tempted to bite over their general incompetence, killing lazy kitchen staff wasn't part of my general operations.

I only killed people who deserved it, after I vetted their guilt and methodically researched their methods. Then I came up with a plan to make them suffer as their victims had suffered. My way worked; twice, the police had marked the wrong people as the killers, and I'd found the truth poking my serpentine nose where it didn't belong.

Those jobs had been the hardest, as I championed the

innocent while proving without shadow of a doubt the guilt of my victims.

Headlines of the slayings haunted me for months after each of those hits, making the national American news. There'd been an entire episode of a crime show dedicated to one of my murders, one I watched with glee. The show writers had *almost* gotten it right—almost. They had painted me as a man.

Me, a man? By default, I broke the rule about being a model-pretty princess, although I could pass muster with my mother when I pulled out all the stops. I wasn't ugly, but I wasn't pretty in the traditional sense, either. My mother liked telling me I was a queen without a kingdom, the cold beauty of a sword unsheathed for battle and destined for conquest.

Her Royal Majesty really needed to stop thinking about conquering things all the time, using me as an excuse to do it. I sure as hell couldn't inherit *her* kingdom. I could barely swim. I supposed she conquered islands across her territory to give me a place to rule from, should she die or make a run for the hills. Fortunately for me, mermaids lived a long time. My grandparents and *their* grandparents still lived, happy to have abdicated their crowns to the next in line. After a few hundred years of putting up with the bullshit involved with ruling a kingdom as vast as theirs, I didn't blame them for ditching the job.

I counted my blessings they hadn't visited me in years. I'd been five the last time I'd seen them, and as I was no longer interesting to them, they went about their business and left me to mine. Of course, Her Royal Majesty had trusted them to watch me for a whole week and they had left after the first day. Maybe that had something to do with them no longer visiting me. My mother hadn't been happy about that for some reason.

I thought my grandparents had had the right idea. They had bored me, I had bored them, so it made sense they had gone to find something better to do with their time.

I spent the rest of my wait considering therapy, coming to the conclusion I probably needed a psychiatrist far more than my mother. I *did* have a rather gruesome hobby of killing people. All she did was conquer small islands so I could live on them. Most of the islands didn't even have inhabitants. Well, the one did, but the tourists had found the whole hostile takeover amusing, especially when the ladies discovered mermen were infertile except during spawning season.

When in human form, mermen liked prettying themselves up almost as much as they enjoyed sharing a bed with human women.

Overnight, my island had gotten very popular for some reason. I supposed I needed to thank my mother for conquering a profitable place for me to live; the resort was like a palace, although most of the staff had no idea I was actually a princess. When I was perfectly honest about it, it was one of my favorite places in the world, and I even booked my own room pretending I didn't have the best suite all to myself if I wanted it.

Unfortunately, it was also a favored spot for the mermen to visit, and once one of them saw me, they blabbed. I suspected they'd helped my mother enforce one of the more annoying chapters in the Modern Guide to Being a Princess, the one that insisted princesses remain virgins until married.

That rule my lovely mother had broken by having me in the first place, as she didn't have a ring on her finger, not that mermaids wore rings. Mermen marked their territory with their teeth, leaving a nice set of scars on their mermaid to declare she belonged to someone. The mermaids left their marks, too—and enforced their claim with the threat of biting off something most mermen were rather fond of.

I was almost a hundred percent certain no one had gotten their teeth on my mother. Almost. If someone had, he'd put his teeth somewhere rather private, and if so, I didn't want to know anything about it.

Did the kitchen have any poison? Indulging in a large swallow of some toxic substance seemed a lot safer than thinking about my mother like that.

Fortunately for me, before I could continue my downward spiral into parent-induced insanity, the kitchen staff finished cleaning, and one of them took my cart on a stroll. I kept my coils lifted, safe from the wheels, and watched the floor so my scales wouldn't rasp against the tiles. An elevator took us to the ground floor, and from there, to an indoor garage, up a ramp, and into a waiting truck.

I would've thought anything dealing with food would've been transported in a refrigerated vehicle, but I ended up packed in with a bunch of boxes, the humid air smothering. Waiting until several men shut the doors, I untangled myself from the frame and explored my getaway truck. A lazy packer meant lots of spaces between the boxes, and I hid behind a few, close enough to the doors I could make my escape at the first opportunity, but not so close I'd be spotted.

For not actually having a plan, it had gone off without a hitch. Hissing my satisfaction, I settled in to wait. The truck bounced and rattled as it increased its speed. Within a few minutes, the driver killed the engine, someone opened the back, and promptly wandered away.

I was surrounded by idiots.

Darkness and rain-slicked asphalt greeted me, and I bailed from my getaway vehicle, lifting my head for a better look around. I darted across an empty parking lot to where it met the curb, hissing my displeasure at the miserable weather. Once on the grass, I coiled up and took a better look around.

I recognized the discount fruit and vegetable market, a hefty hike from my apartment. It would take me the better part of two or three hours to reach Lake Superior's shores near my home. Hissing my discontent, I went about it, determined to sleep in my own bed and lick my wounds—and toss back a few painkillers to banish my headache.

The entire way, I kept close to the curb and used my dark gray body to hide in the shadows and avoid drawing attention to myself. Most times, I rather enjoyed my length, but when I wanted to be subtle, I envied average black mambas, which averaged between six and nine feet long. Fortunately, the streets were mostly empty, and I pegged the time at between two to four in the morning. At four, the morning rush hour started, and I definitely didn't want to be caught outside when dawn came.

Sometimes, I really hated Minnesota. No matter what time of year, when it rained, it got too cold for me, and it didn't matter if I had skin or scales. By the time I reached the two-story apartment building several blocks from the water, I wanted to hibernate for a month. Hibernation, however, wasn't in the cards.

A pissy Terrance stood on my doorstep arguing with my

suspected father, one Mr. Shiny Shoes, who I recognized from his snakes and his wet, shiny shoes.

A brief eavesdrop informed me Terrance refused to indulge in Mr. Shiny Shoes's base desire to petrify my front door and smash his way inside. I'd have to make my mother give the merman a raise. Petrifying and smashing my door in would lose me my security deposit, and if they cost me my security deposit, I'd be pissed.

So much for heading to my nice bed, popping painkillers, and taking a nap. At least I'd get the jump on them. I took the long way around to the back of the apartment building, climbed the rain spout, and entered my apartment through a two-inch hole I'd drilled through the wall behind the pipe and had covered with several metal plates I could nose out of the way to let myself in and out as I pleased. Infiltration complete, I went into my bedroom, shifted, quietly changed into my pajamas, and tip-toed my way to my front door to listen to the two outside devolve into one-word, single-celled amoebas.

Men. Why couldn't they expand their discussion beyond childish yes and no battles of stubborn pride? Under the cover of them snarling at each other, I unlocked my door, yanked it open, sided with Terrance, and barked, "No. Go away. You'll wake the neighbors *and* the dead down the block."

I shut the door with a firm thump and engaged the locks —both of them.

"Princess Tulip!" Terrance must have been reading the Modern Guide to Being a Princess, too, as he had mastered wailing.

"Have you been in there the whole time?" Mr. Shiny Shoes demanded.

"Are you going to stay out there and bother me all night long if I don't let you in?"

"Yes," both replied.

I thought about it, and ultimately, curiosity got the better of me. Unlocking my door, I opened it just enough to indicate they could enter. "Fine. But if you even think about dragging me back to that prison, I'm going to test out how many of my mother's stupid rules I can break in five minutes."

"Haven't you broken enough of them for one day?" Terrance complained, stepping inside before dipping into a short bow. "Your Highness."

"You fucking owe me a lollipop, Terrance. I'm pretty sure you're the reason I didn't get one."

Mr. Shiny Shoes followed my mother's head of security into my apartment, and unlike the first time I'd seen him, his black mambas draped over his shoulders, snoozing as far as I could tell. Lucky bastards. I'd show them all I was a better black mamba. Maybe Mr. Shiny Shoes had a baker's dozen, but I could eat his for breakfast.

"Really, Your Highness? You don't need a lollipop." Terrance took a long look at my living room, most of his attention focusing on my couch and coffee table, which still had the ruins of my breakfast on it. "You need a maid."

Shooting the merman a glare, I snatched the dirty plate, scraped it, and dumped it in the sink along with the rest of my dishes. At least they didn't smell—I'd made a point of rinsing them off with dish soap before my ill-fated outing to kill my target. My close proximity to my sink put me in easy reach of my dart gun, which could deliver enough sedative to take them out far faster than they could react. I even had some rather lethal ones hidden around in case of emergency.

I hadn't enjoyed the process of milking my own fangs for venom, but I found the results worthwhile.

"It's not like I was expecting company *or* a mail bomb today," I countered, opening the door beneath the sink to get my dish gloves and my dart gun. Temptation, thy name was Terrance—and dear old dad, who had purchased me from my mother for a dollar. Death was too good of a fate for my parents, so I'd enjoy a long life of torturing them, beginning with a little humiliation. Thus armed, I slapped the rubber gloves to the countertop. "In case it has slipped your notice, I'm an adult."

"You're a mailman." Scorn dripped from Terrance's words, relieving me of any guilt from what I was about to do to him. "You have been caught in the blast of what, five mail bombs now? You're not just a mailman. You're a cursed mailman."

"I prefer the term courier." I faked a sniffle. "At least make sure the door's locked if you're going to be bothering me. I've got enough of a headache without having to worry about any unwanted visitors."

Mr. Shiny Shoes turned to check the door, and his movement drew Terrance's attention away from me.

If Terrance found out how many hours I'd spent at a gun range over the years, he would've been proud of me. One dart would fully knock someone out within a minute or two, rendering them helpless within a few heartbeats. I nailed both men in the shoulder, smiling while they stiffened. So close to the brain, it wouldn't take long for them to fall prey to the drug. Terrance even managed to raise his hand to reach for the little dart embedded in his skin, swaying on his feet. With dart gun in hand, I strolled to them, ready to help them to the floor so they wouldn't get hurt.

Mr. Shiny Shoes almost managed to turn before he slumped, and I caught hold of his suit in a fisted hand, easing his descent. Terrance didn't last much longer, and I caught most of his weight with my shoulder, kneeling between them and chuckling softly while they fought to retain consciousness.

I smiled and patted my mother's head of security on the cheek. "Next time, remember I'm a big girl, ne? Nighty night, Terrance." Sliding my gaze to Mr. Shiny Shoes, I waved. "Nighty night to you, too, Mr. Shiny Shoes. Nice meeting you. Have a nice nap."

I GAVE my victims five minutes to make certain they were fully under before I went to work. First, I removed the darts and checked the wounds to confirm they weren't bleeding much. Once confident I hadn't done permanent damage, I relieved them of their jackets and unbuttoned their shirts. As far as sedatives went, the one I favored packed a punch, but it tended to make my victims sweat. Partial nudity would be a lot more comfortable for them, and it'd make them both ask questions. After I dragged them in front of the air conditioner to keep them cool until they woke up, I drew little kisses on them in bright red lipstick to add to their morning dose of panic.

To my relief, both kept their cell phones and wallets in their jackets, and I relieved Terrance of four guns so he wouldn't shoot someone—me—when he woke up. Suspicious, I patted him down and even checked his shoes, discovering a little derringer hidden in his sock.

Sneaky Terrance. I claimed the tiny, one-round gun as punishment for letting me get the drop on him so easily.

I gave them both a check over, timed their pulses, and determined they would emerge from sedation without issue. I had a counter handy if something went south, and I even had a few emergency tricks up my sleeve, but I preferred a slick, clean job—one that didn't result in my victim needing a trip to the hospital.

The people I sent to the hospital arrived in body bags.

I began with Terrance, checking through his cards and cash for anything of interest. I found two copies of my birth certificate, both marked with the Flandersmythe family seal and a sunburst seal, except the rays were serpent heads. After meeting Mr. Shiny Shoes, I had no doubts they were meant to depict black mambas. According to the paper, my father's name was Rufus Dimitri Calens, and I'd never let him live it down.

Rufus was about as bad as Tulip, and if I found out he had anything to do with my name, he'd suffer for eternity. Taking Mr. Shiny Shoes's wallet, I sifted through the cards until I located his driver's license. Sure enough, I held the identification of one Rufus D. Calens, resident of South Dakota.

How sweet, hopping over the Minnesota border to see me wearing a hospital gown, daring to smugly inform me my ways of escape were blocked. He deserved a good sedation. Like Terrance, dear old dad had a copy of my birth certificate folded in his wallet. The five pictures caught me by surprise, though. One from when I'd been a baby, three had been taken upon discovering my mother had conquered another island, capturing my speechless fury, and the final one was of me arguing with my mother. Judging from the copy of her precious little handbook in my hand, it had been taken over Christmas.

A closer inspection of his wallet determined my father had three black credit cards, the type without a spending limit reserved for disgustingly wealthy people. Great. My mother had sold me for a dollar to a guy who didn't need a single one of her pennies. A phone rang, and I fished out my father's phone from his coat.

According to the display, it was one of his security people, Justin Brandywine.

Hello, opportunity. So nice of it to give me a call. Sliding my finger across the display, I answered, "Hello, Mr. Brandywine."

Startled silence, then a barked demand, "Who is this?"

"Don't be too concerned, Mr. Brandywine. I'm not holding your charge hostage or for ransom. He just needed knocked down a few pegs. I thought I'd answer his phone for him while he was taking a little nap. I suppose if it makes you feel better, I could hold him for ransom?"

The long-suffering sigh on the other end of the line was music to my ears. "I'd like to verify Mr. Calens's safety before we continue."

I grabbed Terrance's phone and tested his old passcode, which still worked. "I should be scolding you for leaving him unattended. Really. You do him absolutely no good if you aren't nearby."

"Who says I'm not?"

"I do." The pops from my dart gun were noisy enough anyone nearby the property would've heard them, although they were far softer than the concussive blast of gunfire. Anyway, I'd checked around the complex while sneaking in, and if he'd been on the block, I would've spotted him. "He ran away, didn't he?"

My father's security officer heaved another long-suffering sigh.

"I'll text you a picture in a moment. Could you please give me a number to send it to?"

He did, and I chuckled when Justin's name showed up in Terrance's contacts. So much humiliation in so little time. How could a girl resist? To make it perfect, I moved my father until his head rested on Terrance's chest. I took my time arranging his serpents, braiding them together. Just to be a bitch, I dabbed lipstick to the tips of their little noses. Only then did I snap a photograph of my sedated prizes.

"Sending a picture now."

"From Terry's number, I see." There was a startled silence, then my father's guard laughed long and hard. "To answer your question, yes, he ran away. I assure you, you wouldn't have gotten away with that had I been on duty."

Poor Mr. Brandywine. Had he been present, he would've been the first I had taken out, as much of a threat as the gorgon —if my father decided to petrify me. I probably deserved it. "Do you really want him back? If he ran away, he seems like trouble."

Since my mother had sold me to my father, I thought selling my father back to his security detail was appropriate.

"That would be preferable. Otherwise, I'd have to rescue him."

"Help a lady out here. If you had to rescue him, how humiliating would it be for him?"

"Very."

"If I give you an address and leave the door unlocked, can you humiliate Terrance, too?"

"Arrangements could be made."

"With pictures."

"That seems probable."

"I think this may be the start of a beautiful relationship, Mr. Brandywine. I'll sell your charge to you for small fee, copies of all photographs, and future blackmail material."

"Before I agree to anything, I would like to know who I'm speaking to."

"According to the latest rumor, my mother sold me for a dollar. I'm very offended, as I'm worth far more than that."

"Ah, I see. Everything becomes clear. Good evening, Your Highness. It's a pleasure to finally be able to speak with you. I believe I have a better understanding of the situation now. Her Royal Majesty had called, informing us you had become indisposed."

"I am definitely not indisposed. I escaped from the hospital at my earliest opportunity and found these two men at my apartment."

"Of course, Your Highness."

"How much is he worth, anyway?"

"Should the Calens family agree to pay a ransom, you could probably get several million for your father without having to negotiate. If you're a good negotiator, I suspect you could get more for him. There are other factors, of course."

I cast a doubtful look in my father's direction. "Is he really worth that much?"

"I'm afraid so, Your Highness."

"You can rescue him from my apartment." I gave my address and grumbled a few curses. "I'll leave the key in a magnetic holder underneath the handrail. I'm taking some painkillers and going to bed. I expect breakfast and better painkillers as part of my fee."

"I'll see to it. Thank you for containing him. You'll want to use a lightweight cloth, cheesecloth if you have it, to make hoods for his serpents. A blindfold would not go amiss, as I'm certain His Royal Majesty will be rather surly when he wakes up."

"Noted." I hung up and went to work, leaning the two men together and tying them up. To ensure they couldn't escape, I wrapped their hands with linen, wrapped duct tape around the cloth, then bound their wrists together with rope. A nicer person would have unbraided the black mambas before tying little blindfolds over their equally tiny eyes. I blindfolded them both so Terrance could suffer a bit, too.

Once satisfied neither would be going anywhere without help, I tossed back some painkillers and hit the hay.

Turnabout was fair play.

THE SMELL of cooking bacon lured me from sleep with some help from my landline. I fumbled for the wretched thing so I could fling it across the room. I found its cradle, but my phone was missing. After a few more rings, it quieted, and I heard my mother's grumpy head of security in the living room.

Damn. Someone had woken him, and he was answering my phone. Since turnabout was fair play, I'd let it slide. The presence of bacon in my apartment probably had something to do with my willingness to forgive the merman for answering my phone. With a headache already brewing behind my eyes, I rolled out of bed, grumbled curses, and stepped into the hall and came nose to breasts with my mother.

Nothing soured my morning quite like making close acquaintances with my mother's cleavage.

I took two steps back, the first to escape the cavernous depths of her breasts, and the second so I could tilt my head back and have half a hope of looking her in the eyes. "If you're going to kill me, make it quick, but I'd prefer if you let me have breakfast first."

My mother flicked her bright orange hair over her shoulder, revealing a darker red layer beneath, a reflection of her aquatic half, the red lion fish. When she prepared for battle, she braided her hair so it striped. Planting her hands on her hips, she looked me over head to toe. "You're in your pajamas."

"My house, my rules, and my rules state I wear my pajamas whenever the fuck I want."

"Language."

"That was English, ahou."

"Tulip," she warned.

"That little gem was Japanese." I smiled my sweetest smile. Compared to my mother, who managed to look regal, sophisticated, and beautiful no matter the terrain, I was a newly hatched duck to her peacock. "When did you get here?"

"I came with Mr. Brandywine. Was there any reason you left Terrance tied up in your living room?"

"There is, actually. It's the same reason I left my other guest tied up in my living room." Sliding past my mother, I headed for the kitchen, pausing at the end of the hallway near the living room. Terrance and my father sat on the couch, and both looked rather queasy. The stranger in the kitchen caught my attention, and I whistled, looking him over.

I needed to tip his tailor, because those slacks did amazing things for his ass. Mr. Dreamy had been nice, but I wanted to jump the pretty, pretty dark-haired man in front of my stove. "Hey, Mother?"

"I don't want to know." Strolling into the living room, my mother sank onto my armchair with her usual grace, and from all appearances, she showed no sign of noticing I'd picked it up from a flea market for fifty bucks. It had taken me a month to get all the stains out, but I liked how comfortable it was.

"North America is technically an island, right?"

"A rather large one, I suppose."

"If you feel any urges to conquer landmasses, consider America. They sure do grow pretty men here."

"I just conquered an island, so I don't feel any urges to take over America at the moment."

"Mother, you didn't." Despite my protest, I knew she had. Damn it. I turned to her, leaned against the wall, and crossed my arms over my chest. "Which island this time?"

"Madagascar."

"You conquered Madagascar."

"I was bored."

So many of my queen mother's life choices began with that little three-word statement. Sighing, I shook my head, returned to my kitchen, and rummaged through my fridge for a soda. If I made the assumption the pretty man cooking bacon was my father's bodyguard, he would also provide an escape from my pounding head. "You promised me painkillers."

Without looking away from his work, he dipped his hand into his pocket and held out an orange prescription pill bottle. "Take one."

I snatched it, waged a brief but fierce battle with the cap, and fished out a tiny white pill. I washed it down with soda and returned to the living room. "What are you doing here, Mom?"

"It's traditional."

"What's traditional? Is visiting a foreign nation to get nookie from a gorgon traditional? I'm pretty sure you're just here for the nookie with a gorgon." I cocked an eyebrow and took another sip of my drink. "As far as gorgons go, I guess he's not bad. Nice black mambas. Do you milk them for their venom? If not, you should."

My father's snakes rose from his shoulders and hissed at me.

"Tulip."

"Yes, Mother?"

"I didn't come to America to get nookie."

"Why the hell not? Have you looked at the offerings? America's got lollipops and hot men. Come for the nookie, visit the daughter post coitus. If you're not going to bang His Royal Majesty, at least pick someone and procure a proper heir. It's for the sake of the kingdom. Take a look at me. The only thing I'm fit to rule is my wardrobe, and I'm pretty sure my clothes want to wage a civil war and get the hell out of the union. If you really think I'm going scuba diving to monitor the mer, you're off your rocker, woman. And anyway, you sold me for a dollar, so I'm off the hook."

"You could build a lovely castle on that island I just conquered for you. Give yourself a throne and make the petitioners come to shore for your wisdom. Also, you're not off the hook. You better hope I live a damned long time, little girl. The start of your punishment for working as a mail courier again is remaining my heir. Madagascar, starting in the near future, is *your* responsibility."

Terrance leaned forward, his face cradled in his hands. "I think I'm going to be sick."

I helpfully pointed at the trashcan beside him. "There's a

can right beside you, Terrance. Try not to upchuck on my carpet. It's a bitch to clean. Drink some water and treat it like a hangover. You'll be fine in a few hours." I turned my attention to my father. "Same applies to you. I still like the shoes. Nice oxfords, good polish. Anyway, you're dehydrated, not dying. You should be ashamed of yourselves, letting a dainty little girl like me get the jump on you. You deserved it. First, you let me escape from the hospital, then you let me shoot you in the back. Mother, please consider this my application for independence. Go spawn a proper heir and inflict that awful handbook on them."

"Where did I go wrong with you?" my mother complained.

"You gave me an easy-to-follow guide with directions. Shouldn't you be overseeing Madagascar right now?"

"I conquered it for you. I'd much prefer to conquer England, but the queen asked me not to. She was pretty polite about it. She sent me a lovely pearl necklace as a gift. Pink pearls. You know how much I like good pink pearls."

A knock at my door drew a sigh out of me, and I headed over, jerking it open. "What?"

Mr. Dreamy stared at me, his eyebrows rising. "Miss Flandersmythe." He showed me his badge. "I need a few minutes of your time."

His old man partner was with him, and I waved at him. "Hey, Grandpa. How's it hanging?"

"I'm doing fine, Miss Flandersmythe. How are you feeling?"

"You tell me. My apartment has been taken over by several invasive species. Come on in. Don't mind the clutter." I backed away from the door and let the two cops figure the rest out from there. Returning to the kitchen, I caught my father's delicious bodyguard placing bacon on a paper towel. I snatched a sizzling piece, ignored the burn, and chomped on it.

Heaven truly was a piece of bacon. "I'm taking you home with me," I informed my newly elected chef, grabbing a second piece. "I don't even care what species you are. Your job, from this day forward, is to make me bacon every morning."

"No," my mother, my father, and Terrance snapped.

"Why the hell not?" I shoved the second piece of bacon into my mouth, grabbed two more pieces, and wandered back into the living room. "We're talking about bacon here."

My father's snakes hissed at me, and breaking off a piece of bacon, I headed over, leaned over the coffee table, and jammed a piece into the largest one's mouth while my father blinked and stared at me with a rather stunned expression. "Bacon," I informed it.

Twelve more pieces of bacon later, and I suspected I ruled over my father's serpents more than he did. Unfortunately, it took all of my bacon to feed the damned things, and I licked my fingers, muttering curses I hadn't gotten enough extra for me, too.

"Miss Flandersmythe, about yesterday," Mr. Dreamy began.

I flashed the American my best smile. "What about it? I was on my usual route handling deliveries, although I'd started on the backend first to switch things up a bit—a lot of heavy packages yesterday."

"Did you see anything or anyone suspicious?"

I shook my head and regretted it. Why did headaches have to throb so bloody much? "It was a run of the mill day for me, sir. I didn't notice his body until I was near his door."

"And the bomb?"

"I tossed his package when I found him. I think it landed behind me. That was when it exploded. I didn't see anyone around the house, didn't see anyone who wasn't supposed to be there. Nothing unusual at all."

"What time did you reach the victim's house?"

I thought about it. In order to get the timing just right, I'd planned for thirty minutes with him—a lot less time than I liked for a job like his. The gruesome murder of a serial killing rapist deserved hours. If I could've, I would've spent days torturing Matthew Henders before finishing him off. "I guess around noon? I was doing my route backwards, and I don't normally pay a lot of attention to the time. Call it five after, and that'd be pretty close."

By 'pretty close' I actually meant 'exactly.'

A good murder needed to be precisely timed. I'd even planned a rather embarrassing claim of needing to use the bathroom to get into his house. Of course, I'd expected—no, planned on—him to try to take me as a victim, as I fit his profile. He'd targeted a lot of people, but he liked the ones with haughty expressions—the eternal snob, no matter their actual personality. From my research, he'd been bullied as a child and wanted revenge on everyone who resembled those who'd tormented him in his youth.

"Have you ever spoken to him before?"

"Mr. Henders? Sure. He usually gets a package or two every week requiring signature. Seemed like a nice enough fellow."

"Were you aware he has a criminal record?"

I feigned my best wide-eyed interest. "I'm just the delivery girl. Why would I care if he had a criminal record? He never left me waiting long when I knocked, signed without a fuss, and shoveled his sidewalk in the winter. That made him one of the nicer customers."

The cops exchanged looks, and Mr. Dreamy frowned before his gaze returned to me. "Why did you leave the hospital?"

"You're joking, right? Have you ever had hospital food? *Awful.* They'll mail the papers, and since I made my break, they aren't even responsible for me. Trust me when I say that's a good thing." I took another sip of my soda. "I'll tell you one thing, I definitely wasn't expecting to find a body on my route yesterday."

"We surmised as much, as the neighbors claim you have a rather piercing scream."

"Anything else I can do for you nice officers?"

Mr. Dreamy scowled and asked a few questions that covered the basics again just to annoy me. We did the same dance a few times, and I gave him variations of the same answer so he wouldn't think I was reading from a script. As the conversation progressed, the pain in my skull eased to be replaced with a rather leisurely spinning and lightheaded-ness, the kind I associated with the truly strong painkillers.

When he finished, he sighed. "That's all. If we have more questions, we'll contact you. And Miss Flandersmythe?"

"Yes?"

"In the future, please be aware that kissing people without their permission counts as sexual assault."

"You grabbed my ass, so I think we're even."

His scowl deepened. "Fine."

He spun on his heel and let himself out of my apartment, his partner a step behind him. Once they were gone, I shut the door and locked it. "I don't think he likes me for some reason."

Everyone sighed, even my father and his bodyguard.

I turned my best glare onto my mother and pointed at her. "This is all your fault."

"My fault? How do you figure that?" My mother cocked her head and arched an elegant, perfect brow. "You were the one who decided to stick your tongue down his throat without his permission."

"And he grabbed my ass without my permission. We're even."

"It's true," Terrance muttered, his head still bowed. "He definitely got a good grip on Her Highness before she gave us the slip. I do believe, however, he intended to keep you from running away, Princess Tulip."

Whirling around to give him a scolding proved my undoing. I turned to face my mother's bodyguard. The tiny white pill and my head conspired for some pretty lousy karmic revenge, sending me on a one-way trip to the carpet.

I WOULD'VE FELT a whole lot better about things if I'd woken up in my own bed. While I liked satin sheets, I preferred mine. I also preferred sleeping in beds meant for one person, not four or five. I thought my double sufficed. Queens seemed huge to me.

When I needed to crawl to reach the edge, the bed was too damned big.

It was also too high.

Scowling, I leaned over, stretching down to touch the rug with my fingertips, a few inches shy from reaching it. Green, red, and gold swirled over a blue field, pretty in a chaotic sort of way.

On the up side, my head no longer hurt, so I'd forgive the relocation likely engineered by my queen mother and executed by my father with the help of their security. Waging war against four at once would put my skills to the test. I'd have to conquer Justin Brandywine first; his bacon-making skills ranked him as my top priority. I supposed I'd have to go for my father next, as I had questions for him.

All I had to do to get rid of my mother was show even a hint of interest in an island in a specific location. Given five minutes and a few phone calls, she'd be out of my hair for a while. It wouldn't take much to convince her to take Terrance with her, especially if I made a point of visiting one of the islands she'd already taken over.

Promising to visit Madagascar to convince the locals the mer wouldn't eat them would suffice. A lot of feather smoothing had been required at my resort. What would calming an entire *nation* take?

I'd lose at least three to four weeks doing basic research on Madagascar, its people, and my inevitable responsibilities —responsibilities I'd need to delegate as much as possible while praying I wouldn't get sucked into whatever it was someone did when a nation was dumped on their lap.

My mother really needed to stop conquering islands before I participated in regicide to go along with serial killing serial killers.

That left me with the issue of who had killed *my* serial killer. I could think of a lot of reasons why someone would murder the bastard, although my professional pride demanded satisfaction. Once I found out who'd done it, I'd leave him—or her—a little note suggesting they kill with better style. If the killer was a woman, I'd even consider teaching her the tricks of the trade.

If a man, I'd consider teaching him the tricks of the trade after convincing him to scratch a few of my itches. Maybe throat slashing lacked style and finesse, but the job had gotten done and the killer had beaten me to the chase. That deserved reward.

Then there was the issue of the mail bomber. I wanted a piece of that pie, and I wouldn't be leaving a note. *That* victim would be arriving to the morgue in teeny tiny little pieces, a reflection of my opinion of their bomb. Going to a murdering rapist's house and slitting his throat was one thing, but mail bombs were another entirely.

I'd make an exception to my rule about killing only serial killers, assuming I could find the bastard. Taking out a mail bomber involved more work than my normal hits; serial killers used patterns, which made them easier to track down. In reality, the mail bomber was likely someone out for revenge, which made him or her a one off, something that made hunting them difficult at best.

If I got bored, I'd try.

For the moment, I'd concentrate my efforts on finding a new serial killer to slaughter.

Satisfied with my tentative plan, I slid off the bed onto the rug to discover it was far plusher than I expected. I stretched out, contemplating if I had anywhere in my apartment big enough for it. If I removed everything out of my living room and treated it like a wall to wall carpet, maybe.

Obviously, I needed to explore and find a smaller but equally lovely rug to take home with me. *Then* I would get to the serious work of picking a new serial killer to murder—and the killer of my serial killer. I really hoped he was a man, a delicious American one I could take home and groom into a proper accomplice in crime.

FIVE

Ah hell, I was my mother's daughter.

THE NEXT TIME I explored someone's home uninvited, I'd take some string and tie it to a door knob so I wouldn't get lost. What sort of house had more passages than the Bible? At least they weren't dark passages, although I couldn't tell where the pale light came from. At first, I thought the ceiling was the source, but my shadow clung to me. I scowled, leveling my glare at the smooth stone walls. I should've known not to wander when I'd left the nice wood pancled halls, gone down a flight of stairs, and ended up in a labyrinth.

My mother would love the place. Much to Terrance's dismay, she enjoyed nothing more than getting lost in maze-like underwater grottos, disappearing for days at a time, and panicking her loyal servants so much they hunted me down, ready to stuff a crown on my head if she didn't turn up.

Ah hell, I was my mother's daughter. I pitied the mer; my mother was bad enough, but unless she got her act together, they ran the risk of being stuck with *me*. Then again, maybe I counted as an upgrade for them. I limited getting lost to on land, giving eager mer a chance to stretch their legs, ran a resort the mer loved almost as much as their temporary human partners did, and could take care of myself.

Except when it came to mail bombs. My close brushes with explosives worried everyone, myself included. One was bad luck. Five was luck of the worst sort. Of course, it didn't help I deliberately put myself as close to serial killers as possible so I could rid the Earth of them. Since I could find them, others could, too.

In a way, I made my own bad luck. Maybe my mother was right. Maybe it was time to hang up the mail courier hat and pick a new method of getting close to my targets. I didn't *always* work as a mail courier to gain access to my victims, but I'd done it a few too many times. Next time, I'd aim for a six-month stint as some serial killer's secretary before getting lured into his basement dungeon, where I'd shift and bite the shit out of him before spending the final hours of his life lecturing him about the errors of his ways.

That would point evidence in my direction, as black mamba venom wasn't easy to get.

Then again, where would someone like *me* get black mamba venom? Current belief stated shifters of all stripes came in one variant: mammals. While there were reptilian supernatural, including gorgons, people like me didn't exist. It had gotten me into and out of trouble, often. Since people couldn't shift into serpents, law enforcement investigators didn't consider the cracks and crevices a snake could get into as an actual possibility.

Smaller mammals, including mice, were so rare they were brushed aside as possibilities, too.

I found another staircase leading down, and instead of

turning back and trying to find my way up like a sane person, I took the adventurous route. The air chilled, and a musty odor lingered in the air, strong enough to make me sneeze. A thin layer of dust billowed beneath my feet with every step, deepening as I descended. By the time I reached the bottom, several inches of pale dust covered everything.

The rotten ruins of a door hung on one hinge, which was so rusted I expected the whole thing to topple when I touched it. I pressed my palm to the decaying wood and shoved, and the hinge broke away with a creak. The door smacked to the floor, a gray cloud billowing up. Covering my mouth and nose with my sleeve, I backed to the steps and waited for the dust to settle.

Beyond, a soft glow illuminated everything and chased away the shadows. A ledge overlooked crumbling ruins, the empty shells of buildings stretching out into a haze wafting from a river cutting through the skeleton of a town. The steps carved into the wall were lined with statues of gorgons, their serpents reared and ready to strike. Each seemed poised to jump out of the stone at me, although a second, closer look revealed most of the statues were only of the upper chest, shoulders, and head, the rest waiting to be carved. Some even bore chisel marks where the work had been started but abandoned.

What was finished seemed so real I couldn't help but reach out and trail my fingers across the smooth stone.

A hand touched my shoulder, startling me so much I shoved away from the statue and spun, balling my hand into a fist, ready to break my assailant's nose to buy myself time to escape. Conventional wisdom suggested avoiding goofing around on staircases, as taking a tumble down the steps could lead to a very early death. Jumping on one without benefit of a railing while fifty feet above the ground was tantamount to suicide.

Instead of plummeting to the stone below, I got yanked as though I were a rag doll. Colliding with a solid, hard chest beat splattering, although I needed to chase down my heart, as I was pretty sure it had galloped away. It amazed me the fright hadn't made me piss my pants.

"You seem to have difficulties with staircases," my father, one Mr. Shiny Shoes, muttered.

Lucky me, embarrassing myself in front of the father I hadn't even formally met yet. I straightened, going through the motions of dusting myself off, well aware it was a futile effort. I'd probably be washing dust and grime out of my hair for weeks. "That was payback for the dart, wasn't it?"

"When I get payback for the dart, it'll be something far more elaborate than sneaking up on you. I'm merely an opportunist, and you seemed rather enamored with the carvings. How could I resist?"

Since I would've done the exact same thing given half a chance, I acknowledged his victory with a nod. "That's fair."

"I certainly thought so. Your mother's rather annoyed you gave her the slip this morning."

Maybe I didn't have a whole lot of experience with having a father, but even I recognized trouble on the horizon. "Mother recruited you to drag me back in chains because you bought me for a dollar, so I'm your responsibility. Also, if you were actually involved in the process of picking my mother as a participant in your evening activities, I question your sanity, although I do rather like existence."

"I see someone was snooping in my wallet and found her birth certificate."

I checked his feet, and while layered with dust, he still wore shiny oxfords. "I may call you Mr. Shiny Shoes for the rest of my life."

"It could be worse, I suppose. I do have a name."

"I saw while snooping in your wallet. It's almost as bad as mine."

"I hadn't known you'd been born or named until your birth certificate arrived in the mail, so you only have your mother to blame for that."

"Oh, that was harsh. Didn't even call you?"

"She preferred taunting me with pictures sent every few months and thorough descriptions of all the trouble you've caused her."

"That sounds like something she would do. Have you considered posting maps of this place in your guest rooms? I might not have gotten lost with a map."

"Most people would've had the common sense to turn back when discovering they'd found a maze of tunnels."

I lifted my chin. "Where's the fun in that?"

"For the record, had I been responsible for naming you, you would've been named Stephanie."

Stephanie was so, so much better than Tulip. I sighed. "Is it too late to have my name changed?"

"I sent your mother a letter asking something along those lines. She told me to deal with it, and if I'd cared enough to name you, I should've stipulated it in our agreement. Your mother's truly frightening. For the record, she paid me a dollar to track you down and keep an eye out for you rather than sell you into slavery or something nefarious like that. She seemed concerned, and rightfully so, you would escape the hospital again. I've also been informed this is the fifth time you've been to the hospital due to something exploding on your mail routes."

"I'm still worth more than a dollar," I muttered. "Anyway, I am, as of yesterday, never delivering mail for anyone ever again. I've learned my lesson. I'll find something safer, like being a secretary. I can't get into too much trouble being a secretary."

My father's black mambas stirred, hissing softly, and regarding me with their small eyes. "I believe your mother's hoping you'll begin handling some of your duties as her heir."

"She conquered Madagascar, so she gets to rule it. When I want to rule an island, I'll conquer it myself, thank you. Unless she's conquering America. I'd consider taking over America."

My father didn't seem very impressed with my declaration. "Why?"

"High selection of good looking men to choose from, for starters." That America had a rather high population of serial killers didn't bother me, either. I really needed to start doing research on my next target—and find a new state to live in for a while. "And no, I'm not allowing either one of you to marry me off or dictate how I spend my evenings. If I want to bang your bodyguard, I will."

My father stared at me, both brows raised. "Shouldn't my bodyguard have a say in that?"

"Is he married?"

"Well, no."

"What's the problem?"

"He's a lycanthrope."

I wrinkled my nose. "Wolf?"

"No, something far more interesting than a wolf."

"So, he's a couple of hundred years old then, infected with a disease, and what else?"

"He's thirty-two, yes, lycanthropy is a disease, and nothing else. I recommend against, as you say, banging my bodyguard."

I crossed my arms and turned away, regarding the gorgon statues while I mulled over his reply. "Elaborate. I want him for his bacon."

"You want Justin for his bacon."

"I am highly motivated by good bacon."

I could feel my father's eyes on me, and if he wasn't questioning my sanity, I'd be very disappointed. "Lycanthropes of all species pick one partner for life. Should you pick him, you're stuck with him, permanently. And then you'd be infected with lycanthropy. Then I'd have to explain to *my* parents why my eldest child and potential heir ran off with my bodyguard."

"Why would I run off with him? If I'm picking him, I'm not going to hide from anyone. I can take responsibility for my actions. His bacon is that good."

"If you want bacon, hire a chef. Also, there's the issue of contracting lycanthropy."

"Immune," I sang out, waving my hand dismissively. "Mom genes and Dad genes—those are yours, by the way— equal no lycanthropy for me. Drives the doctors nuts, since they preach 'what looks like a human, acts like a human, and walks like a human must be a human, and humans contract lycanthropy.' It's really annoying. It could just be a fluke, but I've been exposed several times without any sign of lycanthropy."

Shapeshifting prevented the lycanthropy virus from taking hold, but I preferred brushing it off as some weirdo talent. I'd even undergone some rather amusing tests for the CDC while preventing them from realizing I could shift into a glorious black mamba. I'd even signed several wavers to consent to being exposed to lycanthropy. I'd picked a cougar with all three forms as the disease donor, too. Sadly, I didn't end up becoming a super awesome cat-snake shifter, much to my eternal disappointment.

Black mamba by day, cougar by night. I would've been amazing had I contracted lycanthropy.

My father chuckled. "I seem to have created a freak of nature. Interesting."

"Freak?" I spun to face him, planting my hands on my hips. "Look who's talking. You have snakes for hair."

The snakes hissed their displeasure at me.

"I can also turn you to stone if I want, missy."

Right. I gestured to his pissed off snakes. "Why haven't I been turned to stone yet, anyway? I thought the whole eye contact thing equaled petrification."

"Gorgon males with the proper pedigree only petrify people intentionally. I suppose I should take you upstairs and subject you to petrification, as it's important to note your petrification and reversal times."

I decided to ignore my father's interest into turning me into a statue. "And the gorgon girls with the pedigree? What about them?"

"There are no gorgon girls with the appropriate pedigree."

"Well, that's pretty sexist."

"It's an issue of biology. Of course, some gorgon females are so weak they can't petrify someone unless they put a lot of effort into it, but the magic that prevents me from petrifying someone unintentionally only shows up in gorgon princes and kings. Of course, should a harem queen have the ability, she likely wouldn't use it, as her job is to defend the hive along with her sisters. Petrification is our first line of defense."

"Still pretty sexist."

"You'll get used to it."

"That's what you think, Mr. Shiny Shoes." I turned my attention back to the town below and pointed at it. "Why's there a town underground?"

"Before gorgons were exposed to society, towns like this were how we remained hidden. This was the home of my hive for several hundred years. My grandparents built this town when the Europeans first came."

"Gorgons live for a long time."

"Not always, no. My grandparents were just over two hundred when they passed away. As I'm certain your mother hasn't told you, I'm forty-eight."

At least the math wasn't hard. "You were seventeen?"

Damn it, I hadn't meant to shriek the question.

"Just how old do you think your mother is?"

My mouth dropped open, and I blinked. "Huh."

"You have no idea, do you."

"Not a clue in hell. I'm pretty sure I'm violating some rule in her stupid little handbook by not knowing."

"Sixteen."

"What the hell is wrong with you people? Are you serious?" I wailed, lifted my hands, and yanked on my hair. "I'm the product of teen pregnancy?"

"Arranged teen pregnancy," my father ruthlessly contributed.

"What sort of moron arranged *that* night of debauchery? Because seriously? Snakes eat fish. *Snakes eat fish.* Why would anyone put a gorgon and a mermaid in the same room and not expect a murder?"

"I'm not sure you're ready for the finer points of that conversation."

I glowered at my father, my eyes so narrow I could barely make him out through my lashes. "How many other children do you have thanks to my mother joining you and your gorgon ladies?"

"I see you've already been told the finer points."

"Internet. I looked it up. Also, that's seriously twisted. How many half siblings do I have?"

"None."

My eyes widened. "None? What do you mean none? I thought the whole agreement was so you could have gorgon children. I was just a happy little surprise who showed up later, rather unexpected."

"Shortly before you were born, a disease swept through the Midwest. Gorgons, as well as several other species, were hit hard. My hive was almost entirely wiped out. I survived, my parents survived, as well as two other gorgon kings. At the time, I was still a prince. My father passed his rank to me so he could focus on replenishing our hive." My father wrinkled his nose. "You should be grateful. You're being spared the indignity of coping with countless sisters for the moment."

Comprehension hit me, and I pointed at him. "You're on the market!"

My father closed his eyes, bowed his head, and sighed. "Tulip."

I laughed long and loud, and the sound echoed over the ruins of the old town. "I should sell you for a dollar to see how you like it."

"What worries me about this is that I truly believe you would."

"You figured that out quick." My stomach chose that moment to growl at me. "So. How do we get out of here? I need to hunt down your bodyguard so he can make me some bacon."

"You worry me."

"If I'm just starting to worry you, you haven't been paying attention." I headed for the staircase leading to the maze above. If my declaration to steal Justin Brandywine for his bacon-making skills bothered my father, he'd flip out if he found out his little princess was a serial killer of serial killers. When I got around to dropping him some hints, I'd have to ease him into it very carefully.

Until then, I'd be considering claiming Justin Brandywine. Between his looks, his bacon-making skills, and his well-played revenge with the painkillers, he had potential. Add in his lycanthropy, and he had all the markers of an excellent partner in crime, mayhem, and murder.

SIX

Justin's bacon was worth conquering an entire continent for.

MY FATHER TAUGHT me two things about the labyrinth beneath his home. First, the stone walls had many secrets, and the clever could find them if they knew where to look. Second, the air itself glowed in the presence of those of the blood, marking me, without shadow of a doubt, as his child.

I thought he meant for me to explore the maze and see what I could discover. One day I would, but not until after I found out who had killed my target before I could get to him. If the murderer was a man, perhaps I could lure him into waging a war with Justin Brandywine, and I would favor the winner. Then again, Justin's bacon *was* worth conquering an entire continent for.

Cold-blooded murderer or bacon? Which would win? Who the hell was I kidding?

Murderers were a dime a dozen. Justin and his bacon were coming home with me, even if I had to hire him out from beneath my father's nose. How much would I need to sway the bodyguard's loyalties to me? When my father seemed content to walk in silence, I thought it through carefully.

Would money even sway a lycanthrope? With my haughty appearance and ice queen reputation, he wouldn't be interested in my personality, not unless he found me getting the jump on his charge attractive. He'd probably find my existence insulting.

Security got *so* cranky when someone landed a hit on one of their charges.

"Perhaps you'd like to change into clean clothes?" My father plucked at the sleeves of my pajamas, and to my amusement, a tiny cloud of dust rained down from where he touched me.

"Your shoes aren't so shiny now," I countered. "It's not my fault you didn't include a map of your house and the first way I found happened to go down."

"You could have turned around."

"And miss a chance to explore a creepy tunnel system?"

"I should've known better than to think you might apply common sense to such a situation."

"Next time, I'm going to take string with me and tie it to the door."

My father closed his eyes and took several deep breaths. Excellent. I'd spent less than an hour with him and already tested his patience. If I got a full day with him, he'd be off his rocker before sunset.

"Your mother neglected to inform me we had spawned a devil. I'm also questioning why I haven't petrified your tongue yet."

"You can do that? Just petrify my tongue?" My father's coolness rating skyrocketed. Not only did he wander around without anything covering his snakes or his eyes, he could pick which body parts to petrify? I'd gotten the short end of the gene pool stick. My ability to shift into a black mamba aside, my only real trick was my immunity to lycanthropy, since I wasn't even really all that human to begin with.

"Yes. Your mother might forgive me if I do it, too."

"Might? She'd thank you. She probably daydreams about the day I shut up and do what she wants for once in my life."

"Perhaps it might be best to show you a partial petrification before you deal with the whole thing. Let's just say your mother panicked quite a bit her first time." My father sighed and came to a halt.

"Snakes eat fish," I reminded him.

"I wasn't going to *eat* her."

"Well, I'm definitely grateful for that. I appreciate my birth and all. Also, thanks for not eating my mother."

"I'm not going to eat you, either."

I shot him a glare. "Do I look concerned?"

"No, which is rather surprising. Every other mer I've met was absolutely convinced I was about to eat them. Rather amusing, really. I'm pretty sure your mother thought I was going to eat her when we'd first met, too."

"I don't need or want to know anything else relating to what you did with my mother. I draw the line at the details. Thank you for donating your genes to my existence. Let's leave the details of your contribution a mystery."

He snickered. "Internet already gave you an idea?"

I shuddered at the memory, which had included a very lengthy discourse on what happened from beginning to end, including how many times the surrogate, in this case, my *mother*, ended up petrified. That was a number dependent on the number of female gorgons involved in the mating spree.

"In detail. I think you'll find I've already been sufficiently educated on gorgon mating practices."

"Then I don't have to tell you that there are princes and kings who'd be delighted to have you as their bride."

"They can keep dreaming. I'm more of a one-man kind of girl, and I don't like sharing with other girls." I actually took extreme offense when so-called boyfriends started getting a wandering eye. I could count the number of boyfriends I'd had on one hand, and I'd ditched them all for being a little too happy to look at the other offerings. "I hope you're aware the loyalty of a lycanthrope is *not* a disadvantage in my perspective."

"Anything else I should know?"

"If you give me a handbook on how I should behave for my birthday or for Christmas, I'll murder you with it. The only reason I haven't murdered my mother is because the mer expect me to rule the kingdom upon her death. Fortunately for me, I'm fairly certain her lifespan will surpass mine by centuries, so I should never have to rule a kingdom I can't even visit because I'm not an aquatic. That's why my mother keeps conquering islands, so I can visit the boundaries of her territory."

"Your mother conquered Madagascar."

"I have to admit, that *does* worry me a little. I'm pretty sure Madagascar actually has a substantial population of humans."

"Twenty-five million or so of them."

I choked on my own spit. "Say what?"

"Your mother conquered a nation with a population of twenty-five million humans. There's also a secondary population of approximately five million other sentients on the island. From what I can tell, I think she conquered it because it has some good ocean shorelines suitable for mer spawning. There's also a great deal of protected land on the island. I haven't had a chance to do much actual research, as I was busy trying to locate my missing daughter who had disappeared right out from under my nose in a hospital."

"Oops." I giggled. "That was a work of art, wasn't it?"

"I'm expecting a full explanation of how you pulled that off."

"Keep dreaming."

"All right. Ready for your first lesson on petrification?"

"Not really."

My father turned to me, took hold of my chin, and forced me to look him in the eyes. My tongue tingled, then it started to tickle. Then the tickle intensified into a far more nefarious itch. I yowled, opened my mouth, and stuck my fingers inside, scratching in my desperation to make it stop, which didn't help. Sticking out my tongue, I blew raspberries, which did alleviate the discomfort a little, but not enough for my liking.

"That is not the typical reaction someone has to petrification," my father observed, his tone curious. "By now, you shouldn't be able to say anything."

"It itches," I wailed, giving my tongue another brisk rubbing. It felt like I expected, although I expected it to break out in hives at the rate I was going. To make matters worse, I got a mouthful of dust in my effort to rid myself of the sensation. With tears in my eyes, I tried spitting, but my mouth had dried out so much I couldn't. "Make it stop."

My father chuckled, touched my chin again, and leaned close. After several moments, the itching eased, fading to a tolerable tingling tickle. "How curious. Let's try that again, but perhaps on your hand this time."

I pulled free of his grip and shook my head so hard my hair whipped side to side. "Hell no."

"Or perhaps your feet so you can't run away."

My eyes widened. "I'm not a coward."

"No, you're just a fish. I'm a snake."

Oh hell no. I stomped my foot. "Who are you calling a fish?"

"You."

"Oh, like you're much better with those rat snakes on your head," I snapped.

"Black mambas," he hissed. Then he made with the magic again but, instead of targeting my tongue, the tickling itch raced through me from head to toe. The next thing I knew, I was on the floor writhing in my desperation to make the torture stop, snarling curses and threats while my father crouched beside me, watching with interest.

MY FATHER ROSE to the number one spot on my shit list, and I swore a lifetime of revenge for inflicting so much misery on me for well over an hour. He timed it, fascinated with my reaction to his attempts to petrify me. Instead of turning me to stone, he gave me a case of the itches so bad he had to restrain me to keep me from ripping my skin off with my nails. He kept me pinned with disgusting ease, one foot on my left wrist while he held my right, checking my pulse every now and then while I panted to catch my breath.

"Your nails turned a lovely opal," he commented, turning my hand over in his, inspecting my fingers with interest. "While your mother has limited resistance to petrification, you seem to have taken after my side of the family."

I sucked in several gasped breaths and asked, "What do you mean?"

"Petrifying another gorgon is more a battle of wills. The stronger gorgon will win, but the time it takes for petrification to take hold is dependent on the difference in strength. How long the gorgon remains petrified is also a matter of strength and ability. The weaker ones require neutralizer or magic, while the stronger ones will reverse the petrification on their own given time, usually few days. It's a good way for rival gorgons to settle disputes without death. Consider it a few days in time out for the loser while the victor gloats over their statue. It's polite to reverse a petrification after a week, however. When I attempted to petrify your tongue, I treated you as I would a regular human. That requires a lot less effort on my part. I'll have to ask your grandfather to have a try. He has the finesse of his long years backing him."

"He'd better not. I'll feed his snakes to him!" I strained to pull my wrist out of my father's hand. "Let go."

"Are you going to claw your skin off? Your nails are going to do a little bit more damage than you're used to until the petrification reverses. Wasn't I nice? I focused on your fingernails. I could've done your tongue instead. Are you still itching?"

"I'm not going to scratch," I grumbled.

He released me and shifted his foot away from my arm, and stood. "When your fingernails return to normal, mark the time."

Bracing for the worst, I peeked at my hand. Nail polish wasn't something I indulged in often, although I liked some of the more flamboyant colors. I was no expert in gemstones, but my fingernails had turned a rather pretty blue and purple, and the way the colors melded gave the illusion they burned. "If I notice. Or had something to mark the time with."

Reaching into his pocket, my father pulled out my cell phone and held it out. "How about with this? Also, your boss called, and I notified him you were not going to be coming in to work due to medical reasons. Apparently, he seemed to believe unless you were still in the hospital, there was no excuse for you to miss work. We had words."

"You got me fired, didn't you?"

"I thought you'd prefer quitting over being fired, so I beat him to the chase and informed him you were quitting."

Death was definitely too good of a fate for my parents. "Your days are numbered, Mr. Shiny Shoes."

Instead of displaying the appropriate amount of fear, my father smiled. "Your mother warned me you're rather proud."

"You're lucky I was planning to quit anyway."

"She didn't tell me you were sensible, however."

"Someone in this family has to be." I flung my hands in the air, and more dust rained down from my pajamas. "You *have* met my mother, haven't you? The mermaid who decided it was a good idea to conquer Madagascar?"

"Astonishingly, I have met her. In fact, we spent most of the time you were napping discussing how best to keep you contained, as you seem to attract a great deal of trouble."

I smirked, a rather sinister idea bubbling to the surface. A good girl would have resisted, smothering the impulse. Me? I could get a little bit of revenge against my parents *and* get a much closer look at Justin Brandywine at the same time. "Mother *has* been complaining every time I pick up a boyfriend, I end up ditching the cheating bastard before I can produce an heir. That bodyguard of yours is a lycanthrope and he's young enough. I bet he'd produce a decent heir or three."

"Absolutely not."

My smile widened into a full-fledged grin. "But he's a single lycanthrope. Aren't lycanthropes the ultimate father material? Loyal to death, protective?"

Narrowing his eyes, my father looked me over. "You're doing that on purpose. You're not actually interested in him, are you?"

Laughing, I got to my feet and dusted myself off, spreading the mess around rather than ridding my clothes of it. "I'm not telling."

"It seems I truly did help spawn a devil."

"A devil? Don't you mean *the* devil? And anyway, I wasn't actually spawned. And no, I don't want the details, thank you very much."

"The true irony here is that among gorgons, the fastest way to insult someone is to call them a spawn."

"I'll remember that."

"I was told mer had a spawning season. Is that incorrect?"

Was I really going to have to give my own father a biology lesson on mer? I shuddered. "Two forms, two ways to reproduce. If you want to know more than that, I recommend the internet—or ask my mother. I'm sure she'd be happy to give you the details. If we could pretend this conversation never happened, that'd be great."

"There are several gorgon kings and princes interested in making your acquaintance."

"I'm pretty sure we already went over this. Unless they're coming over to say hi without trying to get me to participate in their little mating rituals, they can go fuck themselves with sticks."

"How eloquent."

"Would it be more polite of me if I provided the sticks? I'm sure I could find a few somewhere."

"No, that's quite all right. I'll make certain they're aware you're not currently entertaining the prospect of joining a hive as someone's bride."

"When you pitch them that, do make sure 'currently' is not used. I'm not entertaining it, period."

"I'll make them aware, but they'll make offers anyway. The opening bid is typically around five million for a single mating. A permanent arrangement is far more lucrative."

"Well, at least you gorgons appreciate a woman's worth. I approve. Still not happening, though. Just because my mother's adventurous doesn't mean I am. Ask any one of my former boyfriends. I do not share, period—and I'm not lesbian *or* bisexual."

"How did two polyamorous individuals produce a monogamous one?"

I laughed at my father's weary complaint. "Magic."

In truth, I lied, but I wasn't quite ready to tell dear old dad I hated the idea of leaving *my* future child adrift. No, when I got around to picking a partner, he'd be sticking around for life, and any heir of mine would have a mother, a father, grandparents, and the whole works. My parents would just have to deal with it.

SEVEN

I stole your body.

JUSTIN WAITED for us near the door leading to the labyrinth, and his scowl made it clear he wasn't happy with one of us— or both of us. I could readily believe luring his charge away would put me near the top of his shit list. I liked the thought of consuming his attention enough I smiled.

Then, careful to keep my tone light and chipper, I said, "I stole your body."

There were so many different ways he could interpret my words, and my father's sigh confirmed the gorgon knew exactly what I was implying—and threatening.

The list of reasons I wanted Justin for myself kept growing, and his ability to glare at me without wavering made its way onto my list. "Thank you for returning him only slightly damaged this time."

"He isn't damaged. He's dirty. A little dirt isn't going to hurt him. If it does, I'm going to suggest a refund or a therapist."

"I'm going to need a therapist," Justin muttered, soft enough I doubted he meant for me to hear him.

Did a more perfect man exist for me? My target recognized he was doomed, which enthused me more than it should have. "Anyway, you should be more concerned for *my* health. He almost knocked me off a cliff."

My father's bodyguard narrowed his eyes, his attention sliding away from me. "Why?"

My father's smug smile made it easy for me to believe his genes had contributed to my tendency to be a troublemaker. "Opportunity knocked."

Heaving a long-suffering sigh, Justin lifted his hand and massaged the bridge of his nose. "Which one of you am I supposed to be protecting again?"

I pointed at my father while he pointed at me.

Not one to allow a perfect opportunity to escape, I redirected my finger, pointing at myself. "I don't come equipped with a baker's dozen of venomous snakes, and I can't petrify people. I also attract mail bombers. If you have to protect me, you need a raise. You should also add a clause to your contract stating you'll be reimbursed for any bacon purchases."

"You present a good argument. Sir?"

"She presents a good argument," my father agreed, shoving his hands in his pockets. "I intend on keeping you, Justin."

"I intend on kidnapping him, taking him home with me, and forcing him to make me bacon for the rest of my life. Since his lifespan—and yours—is probably far longer than mine, you can have him back after I kick the bucket. I'm the jealous type, so I develop urges to stab women when they catch my man's attention. I also wander off at my whim, and I won't be nice enough to notify anyone when I'm wandering." I smiled at Justin. "I recommend begging my father to let you stay with him. A smart man would be begging right now."

The game had begun, and I waited for Justin to make his move. Would he rise to my challenge or play it cool?

"Princess, should I have the misfortune of being assigned as your bodyguard, I'll be investing in a leash."

I would enjoy making him regret that comment. "I don't actually need a bodyguard. I just need to find a better job, which I'll be doing as soon as you contain your charge and get him out of my hair. If you wouldn't mind arranging a rental for me, that'd be fantastic, as I have to get back to my apartment and pay my rent."

My father coughed, and alarm bells rang in my head. Justin refused to meet my gaze. Whatever my father had done, he'd had help from his bodyguard. Neither spoke.

"What have you done, Mr. Shiny Shoes?"

"I may have permanently relocated you here. It's a matter of your safety," my father confessed.

My father would live to regret his decision to screw around with my apartment, and I would need to reevaluate Justin, his bacon-making skills, and his sexiness rating to better prioritize my theft of his person. "What did you do to my apartment?"

"I relocated its contents, which are currently being cleaned."

Oh, shit. If they'd emptied my apartment, my various stashes of illegal compounds would be found; most weren't hidden all that well, within easy reach so I'd have them if I needed them. I'd made some efforts to disguise the truly dangerous stuff, but the vials with my sedative were obvious, as were some of my other tools, like my guns.

I owned a lot of guns. Maybe if I used them to distract from my other belongings, I could cover my tracks.

"My guns don't need to be cleaned," I hissed through clenched teeth. "I take good care of them, thank you very much."

"You do," Justin agreed, lifting his hands in surrender. "Your guns are safe. I looked them over myself, confirmed they were in good working order, and ordered a gun safe on your behalf. There are often children in the house, so all weapons are locked in a safe unless being carried."

"And my dart gun?" I demanded, planting my hands on my hips.

My father pulled his hand out of his pocket and dismissed my concern with a flippant wave. "In my safe. We'll be having a talk about that compound you used, young lady. I don't know where you got it, but you will procure any additional supplies through approved channels. I'm not against self-defense tools, but let's keep your arsenal legal."

The only legal items I owned were my handguns, which I never used on a job. When I needed to shoot a serial killer, I acquired a weapon from the black market and melted it down once done, scattering the twisted remains in a junkyard to hide them.

Junkyards made excellent places to hide things; the police often checked them for incriminating evidence, but once the compactors got a hold of the trashed weapons, it was impossible to get anything of use. Even if they found my tools of the trade before they made it to the trash compactor, law enforcement rarely thought to check the fragmented bits I left scattered around rusting cars about to be pancaked and smashed into tiny cubes for recycling.

"Is it legal to milk your mambas for their venom? I bet I could make a kickass dart with your venom."

"No." My father scowled. "No, you won't milk my mambas for venom. Absolutely not. No."

"I think we should hold proper negotiations about this issue."

"No."

"Where else am I going to get black mamba venom?"

"How about from the supplier of your last batch? As those vials I discovered weren't legal, I disposed of them. Should you acquire more, don't leave them where I can find them. That said, I'll acknowledge your excellent choice of supplier. The testing I had done on them revealed it was very potent venom."

Damn it. I sighed, debating how best to hide where I'd gotten the venom. Money mattered to mail couriers, which offered me a suitable defense. "If you hadn't been poking your nose where it didn't belong, you wouldn't have found it. That venom was expensive."

"You're getting free rent. I'm certain that'll cover your losses. If you get bored and insist on working, arrangements can be made. It's a twenty-minute drive to Rapid City. I'm sure Justin won't mind escorting you to work to keep you out of trouble. That said, I'm insisting on a lifetime ban from working in any delivery capacity."

"I mind," my father's bodyguard stated, his tone cold.

If he made his intentions to avoid me much clearer, I'd be forced to chase him to the ends of the Earth to enjoy his expression when he learned he wouldn't be getting rid of me that easily. Two could play the same game, and I meant to play it far better than him. When I finished with him, he'd be chasing me, and I'd be running to get caught.

Whether he kept me or I made my escape depended on a lot of things, including how far he'd go to prove he'd be my ideal partner. In reality, he had little to prove. His species and involvement with my father in a bodyguard capacity erased most of my concerns.

No, I was the one with a lot to prove, and I'd test the waters with him in the only way I knew how: toying with him.

"Tulip?" my father asked, and I thought I heard concern in his voice.

"I'm busy considering the best way to eviscerate your bodyguard, Mr. Shiny Shoes. Give me a minute."

"You can't eviscerate my bodyguard."

"I thought denying me my request to take him home with me so he can wake me every morning with his bacon was unreasonable. Why ban a good evisceration?"

"I need him alive, as do you, if you want him to make you bacon every morning."

"So, you're saying him coming home with me and making me bacon for the rest of my life isn't actually off the table?"

The moment my father realized I'd cornered him, he spat curses. "My apologies, Justin."

"With all due respect, sir, you're an idiot. Please stop talking."

Yep, I had a lot of work to do. Convincing Justin he wanted to belong to me would be a challenge, one I'd enjoy far more than any murder I'd ever committed. Until then, I'd nettle him and my father. "Yes, Mr. Shiny Shoes. Listen to your bodyguard. He's right."

Both men glared at me, and I smiled my triumph over having annoyed them.

TRUE TO HIS WORD, my father had relocated my property, but he'd been wise enough to bring me my laptop. If he hadn't, I would've begun my revenge immediately rather than lulling him into a false sense of security. A check of the system logs revealed someone had unsuccessfully attempted to infiltrate the system, costing them almost two hours before they'd given up without accessing a thing. I hoped Justin had been the one attempting to hack his way in.

If I challenged him as much as he would challenge me, good things would happen.

Waiting to pursue him would give me the advantage. Until I was ready to make my next move, I'd turn my attention to my real job. I assumed my father's internet connection was being monitored, so I'd need to take care with how I hunted for my next target. Did South Dakota even have serial killers? A quick look at the state map revealed two larger cities and a variety of smaller towns separated by vast stretches of empty land.

To play to my father's beliefs I possessed at least some common sense, I began with some research into Rapid City, beginning with crime rates, dangerous parts of town, and everything a wise girl interested in protecting herself would want to know.

I targeted my searches to maximize my chance of stumbling across links referencing the types of people who'd escaped justice and left bodies in their wake.

Rapid City had grown exponentially in the past five

years, more than tripling its population. A recent expansion of the Air Force base was partially responsible, with the growth of the weapon and ammunition industry in the area ballooning at an alarming rate. Several new munitions developers had opened up shop, bringing in thousands of new workers, their families, and the supporting tech industry.

The clues pointed to the United States fluffing its military again, although I couldn't imagine why. After the emergence, most nations kept to themselves, the playing field changed from the influx of magic. Too many nations had powerful talents, people who could change the world with a thought. Once small, weak countries possessed the strength to hold their own in battle, and they knew it, and so did their once stronger foes.

Wars still happened, most of them raging in Africa, but the heavy hitters, including the United States, Russia, and China, had decided to stay home instead of flaunting their strength. If America decided to take the offensive rather than participate in conflicts as a supporter, the world would change, and I doubted it would be for the better.

Rapid City's rapid growth worried me, and the population boom made it a ripe target for the type of people I hunted. I kept browsing, focusing my attention to the more dangerous neighborhoods, which skirted the booming industrial sector. Since serial killers walked all paths of life, where I worked wouldn't matter until I got closer to the kill date.

Some were easier to lure out than others; angels of deaths gave me the most trouble. In their twisted way, they believed they were helping people by killing them. Those serial killers either believed they eased suffering or they wanted to remove a drain on society. I hated the latter far more than the former, but both stole lives against the will of their victim.

I'd walked away from an angel of death once. The woman worked in a nursing home, and every last one of her kills happened only when her victim was too far gone to save, withering in a semi-conscious haze, unable to communicate, give their last wishes, or recognize anyone around them, already lost to the world in mind while their body lingered.

She hadn't done it for her victims, but for those left behind, family and friends weary of waiting for their beloved's death to come on its own.

Only in her had I seen mercy, love, and respect for the dying.

I watched from afar for any sign of the woman's mercy turning into something more, but she had, thus far, stayed true, walking the straight and narrow.

I suspected she would change one day, and when she did, I'd be ready for her.

I hated hunting angels of death. They preyed on the old and weak, doing what they believed was right in the worst ways.

In reality, if I wanted to find a serial killer in Rapid City, I'd observe the nursing homes first. From there, I'd search through missing persons databases until I found a trend. If I got lucky, the trend would lead to the same killer, and I'd find the link that chained the victims together.

When I found victims through those databases, I inevitably found their bodies, often dumped together as gruesome trophies for their killer's satisfaction. My search for justice would one day get me caught and killed, but I would keep hunting the hunters until there was no one left for me to hunt.

There was no other place for me, no other purpose.

As I had from the first time I'd murdered a man, I knew the truth. I was unfit for my mother's crown and my father's favor, although neither realized it yet. One day, they would.

Until that day came, I would do what I did best.

If I kept woolgathering, I'd depress myself with my inevitable execution, so after taking a few more minutes isolating the safer neighborhoods in Rapid City, I moved on to step two of my plan to convince my father and my future lycanthrope I was as normal as possible for the daughter of a mermaid and a gorgon.

To screw with my father, I searched for work handling reptiles, particularly snakes, and was unsurprised when I found no openings in the city. To screw with my father's bodyguard, I looked into businesses with late hours skirting the industrial quarter, including overnight warehouses needing stock managers and grunt labor.

To make myself happy, I also looked for better opportunities in the business sector. If my mother saddled me with Madagascar, I'd use my work experience to help smooth the way. I also made a point of beginning my research on the island nation to learn what languages I'd need to speak.

The citizens of conquered island nations appreciated when their new rulers could speak their language. To my delight, I discovered the educated populace spoke French, which would make things easier on me. While rusty, I already knew the basics. Malagasy would challenge me, unless I kidnapped a few natives and forced them to teach me their language.

I definitely wouldn't mention such a scheme to my mother, as she'd have a handful of candidates on the next plane off island—at gunpoint if necessary.

Not only would I have to manage a nation, I'd have to keep my parents from terrorizing the locals.

A princess's work was never done, and thanks to the day I'd gone to kill Matthew Henders, my lot in life was even worse than usual. Oh, well.

I'd figure something out. I always did, one way or another.

EIGHT

My mother had the best minions.

THE PROBLEM with searching for a new job after having worked as a mail courier for so long involved my resume. Firms wanting a secretary had no interest in grunt labor, and in a rare show of obedience, I avoided delivery jobs. I had the skills needed to do the job; my mother had made me manage resorts for months before permitting me to delegate to one of her minions.

My mother had the best minions, and if I ever decided to rule, I wanted to be just like her if I grew up. Unfortunately for her, I doubted I ever would.

She was a lion disguised as a fish, strong, fierce, and lethal. Compared to her, I was a flying fish, determined to jump from the waves and soar without getting anywhere in a hurry. I packed a punch in the lethality department, and I liked being a serpent, but sometimes, I wish I'd sided with one of my parents, for better or worse.

The safest way to be a freak was to ensure no one believed I was a freak at all, and I did that well.

It just meant I had to work with limited options. Drumming my fingers on the monstrosity of an oak desk my father insisted was mine to use as I pleased, I browsed for work. I'd thought becoming a secretary would be easy. People always talked about how secretaries were a dime a dozen, always in demand, and the grunt workers of the business world.

Someone had lied to me—a lot of someones had lied to me.

I suspected the sooner I accepted life made no sense, the happier I'd be. Abandoning my budding career as a paper shuffler, I delved into the dark, murky world of number crunchers. I could pull from my resort experience for my resume for an accountant job; I'd filled every damned position possible at my resort for at least three weeks each, from cleaning toilets to bossing everyone around.

Under no circumstances would I become a maid. People could be downright nasty sometimes, and after discovering humans would leave their soiled underwear in the bathroom for resort employees to find, I'd sworn I'd never work in a janitorial position again.

I frowned. Could my resort work help me land a secretarial job if I targeted companies with interests in hotel management? It beat sneaking around under my father's nose to work a delivery circuit again—or retail.

Working in the resort had cured me of my desire to ever work in retail. Given a week, I'd be at high risk of becoming a mass-murdering psycho. By the time the holiday season rolled around, I'd lead the ranks of serial killers vying for the top spot of most victims killed in the shortest period of time.

No, under no circumstances, could I ever allow myself to

work in retail full-time. I'd make one exception: if I needed to work retail to hunt a serial killer, I'd do it, and I'd take out my frustration on my victim.

Ten applications later, and I considered changing my mind about ruling Madagascar.

Humans, especially Americans, overcomplicated things and enjoyed forms way too much.

A throat cleared behind me, and I recognized my father's voice. Scowling, I leaned back in the leather chair he insisted I use. "Yes, Mr. Shiny Shoes?"

"I've been informed if I leave you unattended for several consecutive hours, you'll find some way to vex me and get into trouble. Is this accurate?"

"Does my mother love or hate me? It's a great mystery of the world. If you must know, I was submitting job applications. I haven't had enough time to get into any trouble yet."

"It's dinner time, and as payback for so many years of sending me pictures, there's a seafood feast to be served in twenty minutes."

If my father learned how many points he earned with me toying with my mother, he'd never let me live it down. "Please tell me there's lobster."

"As I'm not an entirely cruel being, there's even steak to go with the lobster."

"Are the steaks those tiny round ones wrapped in bacon?"

"As I've wisely noted your fixation with all things bacon, I'm pleased to inform you the steaks are round and have been wrapped in bacon for your enjoyment."

"Is this what parental pampering is like?"

My father laughed. "I'm not above culinary bribery to

earn good favor with the women of the household—and I'm also not above using it as a tacky revenge tactic. Tonight, I get to hit two birds with one stone."

At long last, I had life figured out. I was my father's daughter. "She's going to kill you, and I'm going to enjoy watching the show."

"I procured a lion fish, have set his aquarium up in the dining hall, and intend on asking if we were going to eat one of her cousins for dessert."

I had no idea what my mother had done to annoy my father, but I admired the viciousness of his first assault on her delicate sensibilities. "When you die, I'd like to inherit your bodyguard."

"It doesn't work that way, Tulip."

"Why the hell not?"

"Because it doesn't."

"Well, that's pretty shitty of you, setting yourself up to be killed by my mother without gifting your bodyguard to me. You're not going to need him anymore."

"Is there a legitimate reason you're fixated on my body-guard?" my father muttered.

"Yes. One, he's American. Two, he's a gorgeous American. Three, he makes excellent bacon. Four, he might have a sense of humor. I need to do some tests to confirm my suspicions, but I'm feeling confident he possesses a sense of humor. Five, he hates me, which makes it even more enter-taining."

"There will be rules of conduct. Under no circumstances will you assault my bodyguard."

"Physically, sexually, or verbally?"

"No assault."

I scowled and spun in my chair to discover the bodyguard in question was with my father, and he didn't look happy at all. Beaming, I waved at him. "Hi, Justin!"

"Are you sure you can't give her back to the mer, sir?" Justin whispered, so softly I believed he thought I couldn't hear him. I played along, widening my eyes, and portraying innocence.

"No assault," my father repeated.

"Very well. I won't assault your bodyguard without his permission."

"He won't be giving you his permission."

"Well, that's disappointing." I sighed and made a show of shrugging, holding my hands up in surrender. "He'll be pleased to learn I'm capable of driving myself to and from work. Despite my tendency to attract mail bombs, I'm a good driver. No accidents, and no tickets. Are warehouse-to-warehouse lines banned?"

"All forms of delivery are banned, from pizza to transport driving," my father replied.

"I could get a flight license and—"

"Absolutely not."

"When I was young, my grandparents left me unsuper-vised. Are you the overprotective father type who'll go to war over his precious little daughter's plight?"

"Yes."

Oh boy. "Then why are you so set against me taking your bodyguard?"

"He's mine. You'll just have to get your own."

"Pass."

My father sighed, bowing his head. "I'm beginning to think your mother was doing me a kindness taunting me with your pictures all of these years. Reality is a cruel mistress."

"You only have yourself to blame. First, you wrote your contract with my mother in such a way she could do whatever she wanted with me. Second, you contributed half of my DNA, so by the standard laws of genetics, half of my problems are your fault. Third, you could have imposed and taken advantage of my rather wild upbringing and adulthood to visit sooner. In case you're unaware, I'm well over the age of eighteen. Technically, there was nothing preventing you from imposing."

"It seems you're correct. I misspoke earlier. I helped breed the devil, not just a devil."

I smiled. "My mother really will kill you for the fish stunt, but if you have eel, she might forgive you, assuming you set the plate in front of you before she goes for your throat. Also, she loves shark. If you so much as give the lion fish a dirty look, I'll be picking bits of my father out of my hair for years to come. Do try to survive the evening. I've been told fathers are difficult to replace, and my delicate, princess sensibilities haven't been utterly offended by your presence yet."

While Justin looked pained, my father laughed. "You're something else, Tulip. Put away your work and come to dinner. I'd appreciate you witnessing my demise at your mother's hands, so when your grandparents come calling and discover I have been murdered for my poor taste, someone can notify them of the truth. Justin runs away whenever they show up."

I narrowed my eyes and looked my father's bodyguard over. "Interesting. He's afraid of a pair of gorgons?"

"Afraid is far too mild a word. The last time they visited, I found him on the roof trying to hide in the chimney."

"If you come home with me, I solemnly swear I won't

subject any grandparents on you without your consent, and if you're convincing, I might add my parents to the list," I offered with a wink.

"Tempting," my prey replied, heaving a long-suffering sigh.

First, I would find out why my father's bodyguard feared my gorgon grandparents. Then, I would decide what to do about it. The task went onto my ever-growing list, and I rose from my seat. "Should I get changed for dinner?"

"What you're wearing is fine."

I arched a brow. "But you're wearing a suit."

"I rarely wear anything else. You'll get used to it."

No, I wouldn't, and at my first opportunity, I'd make some adjustments to my father's wardrobe. It was only fair, after all. If he could change my living arrangements, I could change his clothes. I'd skip the getting mad part of things altogether.

I had a whole new world of terrorizing my father to explore, and I meant to enjoy it.

TRUE TO MY father's word, he had planned an extravagant feast featuring so many fish dishes my head spun. His pet lion fish was a baby, and it lived in a wall-to-wall fishy palace with at least ten other lion fish who ruled over a coral paradise. The lion fish weren't the only occupants, and I had no doubt I'd lose a lot of time watching the aquarium, which housed an octopus and several species of sharks smart enough to leave the lion fish alone.

My mother waited at the table, her arms crossed over her chest and her eyes narrowed to slits. "You're pure evil."

"I've been informed our daughter is the devil, so I can't be pure evil. She is."

"What's the meaning of this?"

My father stepped to the table, picked up a large, battered and fried shrimp, and bit into it, smiling while he chewed. He swallowed before saying, "I'm declaring war, Your Royal Majesty, and I'm doing so with the most extravagant feast of fish money can buy. Our daughter belongs to me now, and should you want her back, you will have to play my game."

"You presume I want her back."

"That's mean even for you, Mother," I complained, sitting beside her and grabbing the nearest plate with lobster on it. True to my father's claim, there was a steak, and everything still steamed, promising it'd been set on the table shortly before our arrival. "If you allow him to keep me, then you conquered Madagascar for no reason. You hate when you conquer things without reason."

"Breeding season is approaching, and the shoreline is perfect for spawning," she replied with a delicate sniff.

"Are you finally going to pick a His Royal Majesty, or are you going to take pity on my father and participate in some interspecies nookie again? If so, I respectfully demand you leave the bodyguard with me and do so somewhere very far away. Madagascar is a sufficient distance. I further request that if you get bitten, as is proper when picking a His Royal Majesty, you do so in private. No one needs to see that."

"Get bitten?" my father asked, his tone mild.

"If you want to claim her, you have to mutilate her, biting her hard enough it scars as a public mark of your claim. In retaliation, she'll bite you back. When you two are done mauling each other, it's accepted you're a couple. The mer take this very seriously, and should you stray, you will find yourself short a few body parts by the time she's done with you. Should you decide to maul my mother, make certain you don't inject any of your venom. The idea is for both participants to survive the mauling," I answered in my chirpiest voice. "Aren't you excited to have foolishly involved yourself with mer?"

"I see you have had a very thorough education regarding the reproductive practices of other species."

"Mother has been hoping I would get bitten for years and carry on the family line."

"As I said before, there'll be no assaulting of my bodyguard."

My mother's stare locked onto Justin, and she hummed while looking him over. "Do you want him, Tulip?"

While my mother's interference hadn't been part of my plans, I'd find a way to take advantage of her. I waved away her question. "It seems I'm not good enough for His Royal Majesty's bodyguard. No matter. I'm sure I could find a male if I really wanted one, one with the backbone to handle a delicate little princess like me."

My mother reached out, and as expected, she homed in on a plate of eel, placing it in front of her. "Defective male," she muttered.

"Be nice to our hosts, Mother," I chided. "I'm going to pursue some secretarial work in Rapid City for some practical experience on behind-the-scenes management of humans. Secretaries get an excellent view of the nuances of human-to-human interactions, which should be beneficial if you insist I become involved with Madagascar. I'll also be practicing my French in the meantime. Perhaps, if you'll be dragging His Royal Majesty to my new kingdom, you might find some educated women willing to teach me Malagasy."

"You speak French?" my father blurted.

I took my time savoring a bite of lobster and steak, wrapped in bacon as promised, before giving my father my full attention. "I speak six languages fluently, and another four passably. My French is passable. It's an unfortunate consequence of being the daughter of a queen who conquers islands so I can live on them. I need to be able to speak to the locals—or to the people living on the nearest shores."

Justin's eyes widened, and his mouth dropped open.

Excellent. Surprising him would keep his attention focused on me, which served me well. I ignored my father's bodyguard and returned my attention to my dinner, wondering how I'd eat enough to justify the amount of food littering the table. The portion sizes were small enough, but I'd still be stuffed to the gills eating my share of it.

"Despite appearances, she's quite educated," my mother said between bites of eel. My father chuckled, picked the seat across from my mother, and joined me in pursuing a plate of lobster and steak.

I pointed at the seat beside me. "Sit, Justin. If you keep standing like a statue, I'll have to eat even more food, then I'll get fat. If I get fat because you don't sit and eat, I'll make you regret it."

My threats needed work, but Justin sighed and obeyed, although he sat stiffly and glared at the food like it'd bite him. Suspicious he disliked fish, I reached over for the nearest plate with steak and set it in front of him. "My mother eats fish daily. She's a predator. However amusing my father thinks he is, the only reason he got a rise out of her is because she didn't hunt the fish herself—and he implied she's prey."

Justin slumped as though the weight of the world had dropped onto his shoulders. "I need a new job."

"Offer's open. You can make me bacon every morning for the rest of my life. Think about it while you're hard at work preventing my mother from killing my father. I'm sure you'll be appropriately challenged."

"There's the issue of assigning you a bodyguard," my father began.

"The only bodyguard I'll accept is the one seated beside me, and only if he's bringing bacon to me in the morning. Non-negotiable. The last bodyguard I had needed therapy."

So many ideas rattled around in my head, and I liked the thought of sending Justin away with my father for a while, giving him time to wonder about me—or forget about me. Either would do. When he returned, I'd surprise him.

And I'd have a chance to see if he was as interesting as I believed.

"It's true," my mother admitted. "He still hasn't recovered. She's got the pride of a queen, and she doesn't need a mere male to protect her. Unfortunately, she views females as competition to be eliminated, so my options for protection are limited. I value my minions, and after she sent the first few bodyguards to therapy, the wise ones refused the post— and I wasn't going to assign a useless waste of air to *my* heir. I suspect she'll settle down once she chooses a His Highness for herself; he might be able to contain her a little. That's my fault. I taught her to be self-sufficient. When she isn't delivering packages, she's capable of taking care of herself."

"I've banned her from any courier work."

"I wish you well convincing her to listen to you. I've been banning her from working as a courier from her first day.

This fetish with earning her keep is downright disturbing, frankly. She won't even take a vacation. It's disturbing."

My father froze, his fork halfway to his mouth. "You're upset you've raised a responsible woman?"

"That's what minions are for," my mother muttered.

Closing my eyes, I inhaled, held my breath, and waited until my lungs burned before sighing. "Just go to Madagascar, Mother, and take my father with you. You can scout the new addition to your kingdom, handpick a few women to teach me Malagasy, and set things up to your liking. I'll visit for a month each year and handle the critical business. Will that satisfy you?"

"For now," she agreed. "You intend to leave them self-ruling?"

"Is there a reason I shouldn't, as long as you have access to the spawning grounds?"

"No, not really."

"Then leave the poor humans alone. A happy population makes for a wealthy and happy queen—and prevents you from having a very unhappy heir."

"Who taught you to be such a pain?" my mother complained.

"There's only one viable candidate at this table, Mother, and that's you. While I'm grateful for my father's contribution of genetic material, *you* were the one who taught me everything I know. Aren't you proud of yourself?"

Heaving a sigh matched by my father, my mother joined Justin in slumping. "No, I'm not."

"You'll survive," I cheerfully informed her before turning my attention back to my dinner. "This really is delicious. You've won this round, Father. Knowing my mother, she might forgive you for that someday. I recommend pink pearls if you're looking for bribes, but you'd better make them good. She'll even delay conquering tempting islands for a string of good, pink pearls."

"Traitor," my mother complained.

I counted myself the real winner of the mealtime posturing session, and content with my victory, I focused my full attention on my dinner while my parents bickered and Justin sighed.

NINE

Had I been a better daughter, I wouldn't have laughed so hard over her flight.

I NEEDED to stop underestimating my father.

While I convinced him to accompany my mother on her adventures, he introduced me to my latest set of keepers, two formidable foes I'd have to be careful around. My grandparents were gorgons, and at their first hiss, my mother bolted for freedom, not even sticking around long enough to say goodbye to me.

Had I been a better daughter, I wouldn't have laughed so hard over her flight.

My father sighed and called out loud enough for my fleeing mother to hear, "They're not going to bite or petrify you."

Snakes ate fish, and no matter how many times my father had likely tried to convince my mother my grandparents wouldn't eat her, he couldn't get through to her. Deeper in the house, a door slammed.

Justin sighed, too. "I'll make certain she doesn't get lost, sir."

"Thank you, Justin."

I swallowed my laughter, keeping still and quiet like a proper princess despite being my father's daughter. Like him, I wanted to laugh and enjoy Her Royal Majesty's discomfort.

That left the problem of my grandparents, who fit the little old lady and little old man profiles so well I wasn't sure what I was supposed to do with them. My grandfather was a lot like my father, possessing thirteen black mambas and the ability to walk around without any coverings. My grandmother's snakes wore tiny little hats with tinier black veils, and her veil obscured all but her mouth.

When she smiled, I considered running for the hills. I'd been bitten by a vampire once, and his fangs had nothing on hers. His hadn't dripped venom, either. I wasn't sure what sort of snakes she had, but they were a rosy hue with diamonds decorating their spine.

"It seems our son produced a cute hatchling with that mermaid of his," my grandfather rasped, and unlike my father, he had a forked tongue. "A pity we didn't get to meet your mother properly."

My father smiled. "I'm sure she'll be back eventually. Hopefully, I can convince her to be a little less skittish around our serpents."

"My father forgets snakes eat fish, and the only good snake in the mer kingdom is a dead one." I smiled my best smile. "It's a pleasure to meet you."

"You don't seem to have inherited your mother's fear of snakes." My grandmother smiled wider, and she licked her fangs. "We've been told you're uninterested in becoming a bride."

"Gorgons are a polyamorous species. I'm monogamous.

It's likely a genetic mutation. Mer are polyamorous unless they decide otherwise. Of course, Mer are generally inclined to form permanent partnerships as part of the mating season to better care for the hatchlings, but it isn't guaranteed. Some choose to have hatchlings without biting their partner."

"I like the sound of that," my grandmother replied, clicking her teeth together. "I enjoy a good bite."

"When a mer decides to dedicate to someone, they mutilate them, tearing into their chosen partner until the wounds are bad enough to leave permanent scars. This is done mutually. Should the couple survive, they're partners for life. Mer talk with their teeth." I showed my dull, human teeth. "Should a male cheat on his partner, she will use her teeth to bite off something rather important to him."

My grandfather and father winced while my grandmother laughed.

"Tulip, please," my father muttered in a strained voice.

"Should a female cheat on the male, her breasts are typically targeted, as it cripples her abilities to reproduce successfully as well. While mer are hatched, they're breastfed, and mermaids will not feed the child of a disgraced mermaid." I graced my grandparents with a smile. "It's important to know, should my father decide to engage in any inappropriate biting of my mother's person."

"Inappropriate?" my father demanded.

I smiled my sweetest smile at my father and waited.

Five minutes later, he threw his hands up in disgust and turned, heading in the direction my mother had fled.

"I think we're going to get along quite well," my grandmother declared. "Don't worry none about your little girl, Rufus. We'll take care of her."

I wondered if my grandmother meant to sound threatening. In another first for me, I decided to show some mercy on my mother. When faced with obnoxious gorgon, running seemed like the wisest choice.

My father paused in the doorway. "No petrification, no biting, no running her through her paces, and no adoption matches," he ordered.

The first three made sense, and I narrowed my eyes. "Adoption match?"

"A hive from Wisconsin has eggs up for adoption. Prospective parents fight for the right to adopt the eggs. The hive had consisted of four members, and they were killed in a car accident. The eggs survived. The prospective parents to survive through the worst beating becomes the caretaker of the orphaned eggs. Your grandparents volunteered to oversee the matches."

My eyes widened. "And how would *I* participate?"

"You'd get to beat the prospective parents—"

I beamed at my father. "Yes, please. I'd be glad to help beat gorgons to a near-death state."

"That is obviously the mermaid in you talking," my father complained.

"It'd be a good educational experience for her if she can resist petrification long enough to fight. We'd have to test to find out how resistant she is."

"She itches, and when she itches, she gets violent and cranky," my father warned.

My grandmother showed off her fangs. "Excellent. Run along, Rufus. It'd be a pity if you let your mermaid escape. It was so much work catching one for you."

"Why do I have the feeling if I leave my daughter with

you, she'll be returned even more corrupt than she already is?"

I arched a brow, planted my hands on my hips, and looked my father over from his hissing serpents to his shiny shoes. "Obviously, I didn't inherit my shining intellect and common sense from you."

My grandfather hooted his laughter, and his black mambas reared up and hissed. "You bred us a feisty little fishy, Rufus."

"I'm regretting I called you now."

"Hindsight is ever perfect, dear boy. Off you go before your mermaid escapes. Your hatchling is safe with us, never fear."

"I was a live birth," I informed my grandparents. "Much to my mother's eternal anguish, as I did not inherit any aquatic genetics. The lack of aquatic genes makes it much harder to rule her kingdom, so she's stuck with me. I'm far better at sinking in water than breathing it."

My grandmother's eyes narrowed, and she scowled at me. "That's troublesome. Very well. Our first order of business is to teach you how to swim. No grandchild of mine will be drowning on my watch."

"I can swim. I just can't breathe water."

"You can't swim well enough," she informed me. "Do you own a bathing suit?"

Was my father a bastion of sanity in his family? If so, I feared his contribution of genetic material was the probable cause of my tendency to kill people I found particularly heinous. "No."

"Then that's our first errand for the day." My grandmother seized my grandfather by a handful of his black mambas and dragged him across the room. "Come along, little hatchling. We're going shopping."

My father sighed. "I'm sorry about this."

"You will pay for your misguided belief that I require supervision, Mr. Shiny Shoes. Go keep my mother from getting herself into trouble. If you were really sorry, you'd give your bodyguard to me instead of foisting your parents on me, but as I see that isn't happening, I'll come up with an appropriate and sufficient revenge for this."

"I was afraid you'd say something like that."

"You only have yourself to blame, Mr. Shiny Shoes." I shrugged, waved my hand in farewell, and followed after my grandparents, curious to discover how a pair of gorgons went shopping without leaving chaos and statues in their wake.

ON A SCALE of one to ten, I had never been so wrong in my life. I never wanted to witness two gorgons shopping again. They didn't petrify anyone, but chaos came aplenty. The twenty-minute drive to Rapid City went well enough, until we reached civilization.

Humans didn't react well to gorgons in a convertible. The first accident wasn't my grandparents' fault; a driver was so busy staring at them rather than the road, resulting in a wince worthy fender bender. Whether to prove they could play good humans or attempting to set a good example, my grandparents waited for the police, gave their statements, and wasted an entire hour while I waited, leaning against their car.

The vehicle won them a lot of points with me. The

convertible had a back seat, it was comfortable, and pretty enough I considered adding car thief to my resume of illegal activities.

The second one was questionably the fault of my grandfather, who treated yellow lights as green lights and didn't have the common sense to yield to the hybrid-form cat lycanthrope. One smashed truck and a busted fire hydrant later, and the kitty was so mad his fur stood on end. He jumped over vehicles to get a piece of those responsible for the dents in his baby.

While fairly certain gorgons couldn't catch lycanthropy, the hissing, spitting feline catastrophe shattered my tenuous grip on my patience. I jumped out of my grandparents' convertible, closed the distance between us, and gave a little demonstration how a delicate flower of a princess could flatten a several hundred-pound man without breaking a sweat.

Ramming my fist into the fanged maw of a pissed off cat wasn't the brightest move, and I deserved to be bitten. Spitting curses a match for his snarls, I drove my off hand into his gut and snapped, "I'll skin you for your pelt, you oversized marmot!"

"He's a clouded leopard, Tulip," my grandmother announced.

The oversized marmot decided he'd had enough of me, spit out my fist and one of his teeth, and tossed me across the street. I hit the sidewalk hard, rolled, and admired the pretty stars dancing through my vision. Everything I'd ever been told about concussions claimed smacking my head into things wasn't a good idea, but how could I refuse such a violent invitation?

The lycanthrope was either going to die, get beaten

within an inch of his life, or otherwise be subdued. I bared my teeth and hissed, rolled to my hands and knees, and lunged forward on a collision course with my new best enemy.

I hit him at full throttle, and we rolled across the road. "I don't care what he is!"

"But I thought you wanted a lycanthrope." My grandmother stepped out of the car and stood over us, her hands on her hips. "Sonny, you mated yet?"

He might've had better luck answering without my fist shoved in his mouth. "Grandmother, we're busy."

"I see that. Why are you picking a fight with a lycanthrope? You're going to get infected if you keep that up. Instead of taking you swimsuit shopping, I'll be taking you to the hospital. Do you like hospitals? We could've done a planned visit instead."

Removing my hand from the leopard's mouth, I grabbed his jaw and shoved his head back so he wouldn't bite my grandmother. "He was going to rip your car apart. I couldn't let such a bad thing happen to such a nice car. You should teach my grandfather how to drive better. Yellow means be careful, and they have a tendency to turn red when you're partway through the intersection. Add in an impatient cat, and you cause a car accident. Think of your car."

"It's best to let angry lycanthropes work out their agitation, Tulip. The car can be fixed. I'm not so sure your hand can be. It looks rather injured. I may not be adept at caring for human infants, but your father is not going to be pleased when I return you damaged. Isn't mauling how mermaids pick mates?"

"No." The leopard snarled, and I smacked his muzzle.

"Enough, kitty. You're not tearing up the convertible. They'll fix your truck. Bad lycanthrope."

The lycanthrope growled.

"When you can speak English, I'll let you go." I thought I was being reasonable. The clouded leopard disagreed, tossing me over his head. I tucked, rolled, and smacked into the pavement on my back. "Or not."

My grandfather sighed. "Are you quite done being used as a toy by the angry lycanthrope, Tulip? While I'm generally pleased with your willingness to engage with beings substantially larger and far better equipped for a fight than you, your father will be quite angry with us if we permit this to continue."

"He was going to hurt the car."

"Instead of hurting the car, he's done an admirable job of hurting you. As you've busted out several of his teeth and he's shredded your hand, it's a safe assumption you're now infected."

"Immune," I sang, waving my bloodied hand dismissively. "Aren't gorgons immune to lycanthropy?"

"Indeed," my grandfather replied.

"That's what I thought. Hey, lycanthrope. Don't touch the car. That car will be mine one day, and so help me, if you scratch it, I will turn you into a rug."

"Noted," the lycanthrope said, rising to his feet and settling into a crouch. "And what about my truck?"

"Take me hostage for ten minutes. They'll either pay you to keep me or pay you to give me back. Use the money to fix your truck. Ideally, you'll request an appropriate amount, because I'll take offense if you get greedy."

The lycanthrope spit blood. "I've learned something new today. The human spawn of gorgon are tough for flesh bags."

Flesh bags? I rolled onto my stomach, got my arms beneath me, and glared. "Really? You call humans flesh bags?"

"You could let me tear the siding off that car. We'd be even, and maybe they'd learn how to drive."

"Or maybe you'd learn not to run red lights, furface."

"It was changing to green."

"Still your fault. I'm trying to be generous here. We can just wait for the cops to show up instead and explain that while my grandfather unwisely drove through a yellow, you ran the red because you were expecting it to change to green." I smiled, and the lights dancing in my vision annoyed a curse out of me. "Take the faked hostage situation. It can be his punishment for causing a car accident with his irresponsible driving."

The lycanthrope sat back on his heels and looked me over, licking his bloodied muzzle. "It's less sporting if it's a faked one."

"They'd probably take offense if it were a real one. Realistically, they'd petrify you and smash your statue to dust. Gorgons have a reputation for viciousness when cranky."

"What do you think you're doing, Tulip?" my grandfather hissed.

"I'm negotiating a non-violent resolution to the problem you caused, old man. Let me negotiate for a non-violent resolution in peace."

"You tossed a five-hundred-pound hybrid over your shoulder and punched him in the mouth. I fail to see how this is non-violent," my grandfather muttered. "I'm sure our friend would've limited his damage to superficial repairs."

I wrinkled my nose. "I see no need to play by your rules. My rules state this is a non-violent resolution."

My grandfather sighed. "Your rules lack common sense and logic." He turned his attention to the lycanthrope. "How much would I need to pay you to keep her? I can't promise she won't escape, and I'd have to take offense if she wished to leave and you restrained her inappropriately, but I'm sure we can come to an arrangement."

"I set a ten-minute limit on this arrangement already," I reminded them. "And I doubt my father would be very happy if you sold me, especially after having just bought me from my mother."

My grandmother's serpents hissed and swayed, but their tiny hats and veils did some serious damage to her lethality rating. "That's true. He'd be quite upset with us, dear. It's not like he's bred any replacements yet. We should wait to sell this one until he's bred another. Although, maybe we should advise him against breeding again. I think we've made a mistake."

I suspected the exposure to my grandparents and listening to me ruined the lycanthrope's mood, as he got up, went to his busted truck, and returned shortly with an insurance form. "Why don't we just exchange information and let the insurance companies handle it?"

My grandmother's serpents settled, and she made herself comfortable in her car. "That's a lovely idea. That'll minimize how long we have to deal with those pesky police officers."

I'd forgotten about the police officers, and I sighed, staggered to my feet, and wobbled to the convertible. "Self-defense. That's my story, and I'm sticking to it," I declared, climbing into the back, careful to keep my bleeding hand away from the upholstery. "Isn't that right, Mr. Clouded Leopard?"

"Of course. We were having a non-violent negotiation regarding the damage to my truck."

I looked the lycanthrope in the eyes, smiled, and said, "Next time, don't drive your truck into a fire hydrant."

"I'll keep that in mind."

"And don't run red lights, even when you think the light is about to change, because let's face it, I'm probably the only person in this country who doesn't run the yellows."

The lycanthrope turned to my grandparents. "Is she always this annoying?"

My grandmother lifted her hands, mimed shaking a magic eight ball, and said, "All signs point to yes."

"Good to know."

The lycanthrope looked like he wanted to say something else, but the police arrived, took one look at my bloody hand and the lycanthrope's missing teeth, and ensured I'd be spending the rest of the day convincing a haughty doctor I was immune to lycanthropy.

This time, I hoped I got my lollipop. All things considered, I'd earned it.

TEN

Lycanthropy is a serious concern.

IN THE FUTURE, I needed to do more research on lycanthropes. Had I done my research properly, I would've known even the felines had puppy-like tendencies. The clouded leopard followed me to the hospital and watched me like I was the main dish at a catnip buffet. A stern no and snapping my fingers had gotten him to retreat to the waiting room while I faced off against doctors eager to prove I wasn't actually immune to the virus. I'd gotten saddled with three of them, and unlike in Minnesota, they took gorgon royalty a bit more seriously.

Judging by the gleam in Dr. Margret Carden's eyes, I wouldn't be leaving her sight until she was satisfied I was in better than new condition.

"Lycanthropy is a serious concern, Tulip," Dr. Carden repeated for the tenth time in as many minutes.

At least she didn't laugh at my name.

"I'm sure it is, for people who aren't immune to it. Go ahead, check my blood. You're not going to find any traces of the virus. I've been exposed before. It's not my fault the CDC won't flag me as immune because they haven't figured out what makes me immune." I smiled for the woman. "You should be praising me. If I hadn't fed that damned cat my knuckles, he would've ripped up a car before possibly targeting people who aren't immune to the virus. That's the trick to dealing with pissed off lycanthropes. You have to surprise them into forgetting why they're angry in the first place. Then their virus settles down and they can regain control of themselves. That's all I did. I surprised him."

"Most sentients would be surprised when tossed by someone a fifth their size. Your self-defense instructor will be proud."

My self-defense instructor was dead, and I'd been the one to kill the bastard, although he'd been good at teaching. He'd targeted his students because he'd loved when his victims put up a decent fight. "I'm sure he would be."

Dr. Carden jabbed me in the shoulder, and I winced. "Your shoulder and back muscles lost that fight, I'll have you know. Multiple sprains, and you're lucky you didn't break something. Then there's the matter of your concussion. I was forwarded your hospital records from Minnesota. Are you trying to kill yourself, or do you enjoy testing the limits of the human body?"

"I forgot about the concussion," I confessed. "My head wasn't hurting at all when I decided the lycanthrope needed to not bust up my future car."

"In the future, let the lycanthrope damage the car. Cars are easier to fix than people. As it is, you have twenty-seven new stitches, a hairline fracture, more sprains than I wish to count right now, and enough bruising you're going to win awards for interesting colorations for the next week or two."

I regarded the splint on my finger with a scowl. "It'll heal in no time."

Being a shapeshifter helped with that. I'd never match a lycanthrope, but I healed in half the time it took the average human. If I needed to push my luck, transforming would increase my recovery rate, too, although I'd pay for my impatience with fever, general malaise, and weight loss.

I'd learned early on being a shapeshifter wouldn't save me from fatal injury; I'd cut it a little close a few too many times to believe myself immortal. I shouldn't have launched a full-out assault against a lycanthrope, but I had several good reasons for my stupidity. The backup of two easily provoked gorgons took the top prize, and the public setting factored, too.

While it hadn't crossed my mind when I'd tangoed with the clouded leopard, I'd built a new reputation for myself, one I hadn't tried before.

It would make my work killing serial killers more difficult, but I looked forward to living a life where people thought I had more courage than sense. It would help me flirt with Justin, too.

If he was like any other bodyguard I'd ever met, nothing would trip his trigger quite like a reckless body to protect. I had no idea how my run in with a rival lycanthrope would factor.

No, I needed to ditch the kitty, because the kitty wasn't the one I wanted. I wanted the man with the courage to stand up to black mambas and gorgons without breaking a sweat. I wouldn't even hold Justin's fear of my grandparents against him.

Any sane man would have a healthy fear for those two. They put me on edge wondering what they'd do.

I didn't like men like the clouded leopard. Infection with the lycanthropy virus put him a step up from others like him, but if I caught his interest so easily, he'd lose interest just as readily. The lycanthropy virus could transform even the wildest swinger into a loyal husband, but it took time, and I deserved better than a wandering eye.

I needed a challenge, and I needed someone who loved me despite of—and because of—my myriad of flaws. That meant showing him my bad side out of the gate, challenging him, and emerging the victor regardless.

And I needed to see his bad sides, too, and emerge on the other side still wanting him.

So far, I liked what I saw in Justin.

The clouded leopard had temper and fire, but he lacked something, although I wasn't sure what.

"Miss Tulip," Dr. Carden complained.

"Do you think no is enough to deter the leopard outside? Because I don't want him, Dr. Carden."

"As soon as it's proven, without evidence of a doubt, that he hasn't infected you with his virus, I'm sure no will be a sufficient answer. I'd like to remind you, Miss Tulip, that lycanthropes are very serious about mating, and should he have infected you, a single female, he will become a permanent attachment. The infection will ensure your acceptance of him as well."

"Then it's a really good thing I'm immune. While I'm interested in a lycanthrope, he isn't the one I'm interested in."

"You don't have an immunity rating with the CDC, Miss Tulip."

I held out my arm. "Go ahead. Test me."

"It takes three days—"

"I'm telling you there's no point in waiting three days, because no matter which scanner you pull out, I'm going to test negative for the virus."

"It's only been two hours since exposure, Miss Tulip." Dr. Carden frowned at her collection of gadgets, picking one up. "I do have a high sensitivity scanner that's capable of detecting contamination, but two hours isn't sufficient to remove contamination, even among the immune."

I kept my arm lifted for her. "I break the rules."

"I find that highly unlikely."

"Then you'll enjoy gloating should the test show contamination, Dr. Carden. What looks like a human, talks like a human, and looks like a human isn't necessarily human. My father's a gorgon. My mother's a mermaid. Neither species is human."

"According to your file, you have human genetics."

"Yes, yes, over fifty percent, so I'm a human in the eyes of the law. That doesn't change the fact I'm not really a human, Dr. Carden. I'm immune to lycanthropy."

"Then I suppose the tests will decide that." The doctor scowled, but she started the scanner. "Your insurance company isn't going to be pleased with this."

"And they'll approve the scan because it's going to show clean, which means they don't have to pay for lycanthropy monitoring. How many times will I have to repeat myself before someone believes me?"

"When the CDC flags you as immune, I suspect."

Within ten minutes, the doctor had her verdict. I scanned clean, and I even took the high road for once in my life, not saying a word while Dr. Carden confirmed the results three additional times because she couldn't believe what her machines were telling her.

"You've made your point," she conceded.

"Let's cut a deal. You let me out of this joint with this annoying little splint, I'll promise to wear it until the break heals, and we forget this ever happened. Sound good? And you'll make sure that lycanthrope leaves me alone. He's not my type."

"What kind of lycanthrope is your type, dare I ask?"

"He's a bodyguard, he makes the best bacon I've ever tasted, and I'm sure I can convince him to give me the time of day eventually."

Dr. Carden sighed. "He hates you, doesn't he?"

"Hate is such a strong word. I like to think of him as sensible and appropriately cautious about involving himself with a woman like me."

"Are you insane?"

"Honest," I countered.

Dr. Carden's eyes widened. "What do you mean by that?"

"What you see is what you get, Dr. Carden. I prefer to let people judge me on who I actually am. I see no need to dance to the contrived social rules. As I don't play the social game like people wish me to play it, I suppose you could call me insane. I value honesty. I also value enjoying my life and living it to the fullest."

I smiled my way through the worst of lies, as my best kept secrets were hidden right beneath the noses of my victims and pursuers. A paper-thin veneer of lies shrouded me, and all it'd take was a spark to unveil everything, which was why my methods worked so well.

No one wanted to believe the crazy girl next door was actually crazy, and no one liked believing a killer walked among them. That I only killed the other killers meant little.

I still killed.

"You're a very interesting woman, Miss Tulip. As I suspect you'd escape from my hospital like you did the others, I'll agree to your terms under a few conditions."

"What conditions?"

"You'll come back for a checkup within the next two weeks, you will refrain from playing with other lycanthropes, even if they wreck your grandparents' car, and you'll avoid any injuries to your head. A mild concussion can turn into a serious problem if you're not careful. Do we have a deal?"

"Deal," I replied, saluting the doctor. "Do I get a lollipop for good behavior?"

"If you show up to your appointment without having done additional damage to yourself, I might be able to locate a lollipop for you."

"Then I'll see you soon, Dr. Carden."

THE CLOUDED LEOPARD waited with my grandparents, and I looked him over head to toe, flashed him my best smile, and waved the paper declaring I wasn't contaminated in his face. "You're officially in no way responsible for me, Sir Kitten. You can go home with no fear you'll be stuck with me. Trust me when I say this is a very good thing."

"And here I thought I'd be able to enjoy your company for at least three days," the kitty growled, and his ears flattened.

I shouldn't have been surprised a lycanthrope would find having his teeth bashed in by a woman attractive. "I'm sure you'll find a pretty lady who wants to make someone purr at night. That is not me, for the record." Since I had no doubt my grandparents would want to see proof, too, I handed the sheet over to my grandfather. "I'm free to go, but I've been told I should avoid punching any more lycanthropes in the face for at least a week"

"Your doctor is a wise woman," my grandfather replied, looking over the sheet. "All right. Since the target of your affections is out of town, I suppose I don't have to warn him he might be assaulted this week."

"I wouldn't say he's the target of my affections." I shrugged. "Affection is such a flimsy word. I'm hunting a lifetime supply of the best bacon I've ever tasted. That's serious business, old man."

"How would you feel if I told you I taught him how to make bacon?" my grandfather replied.

"You will ensure I'll visit as long as you promise to make me bacon. It's very simple."

"So, if I want to introduce you to prospective grooms, I need to teach them how to make bacon first?"

I shook my head. "You're going to have to try harder than that. My target has checked off every single one of my boxes in the pro column, and he hasn't accumulated any cons yet." I turned to the leopard. "Sorry, kitty. I'm taken, and the taker doesn't know it yet."

"I'm not sure if I should be jealous or relieved," the lycanthrope admitted.

"Go with relieved. That choice is safer for your health."

"You're an unusual woman, Tulip."

"I blame my unique blend of genes for that. I'm what happens when you mix predator and prey species. Snakes eat fish, and while mer *are* predators, when it comes to gorgon, they count as a prey species. It's ugly. I recommend against doing that. Find yourself a nice wolf. The battle between cats and dogs will keep you amused for the rest of your lives."

"You assume finding an interested wolf is easy."

I raised both my brows, planted my hands on my hips while ignoring the pain from my broken finger, and replied, "Nothing worth doing is easy. If it were, everyone would be happy. There's nothing wrong with having higher standards, especially when you're picking a partner for life."

Without waiting for a reply, I turned to my grandparents. They rose from their seats and headed towards the exit, and I followed them without looking back.

Some would call me a bitch for treating the lycanthrope as I did, but I deserved better, and so did he.

MY STUNT PUNCHING an infuriated lycanthrope landed me a pair of infuriated gorgon grandparents, and the instant we reached the car, their serpents scolded me with hisses.

My grandfather took point, narrowing his eyes, and getting in my face. "Care to explain that?"

"Saving my future car from a beating. I already said that. One day, this car will be mine, and I was protecting it. If I'd let that overgrown pussy cat get a hold of it, it would've been crunched like a tin can."

"You're a lot less durable than my car. It's also not going to be your car. I intend on living so long the car rusts apart before I get rid of it."

"You'll upgrade, and when you do, I'll be waiting."

My grandmother crowed her laughter. "She has you there, dear. I fear she takes after our son. We should be grateful she's made it easy to understand how to earn her affections. You need to feed her bacon and agree to give her the car. You'll replace this one as soon as you get tired of it.

Frankly, I'm surprised you've been loyal to this one for a year. You usually last six months before you find a new toy."

"I haven't felt like doing a gemstone run lately. No gemstone runs, no new cars. We've been over this before."

"Gemstone run?" I asked, sliding into the back of my future car. "Is that how you make your money? You mine gemstones?"

"Mine implies he works for it, dear. He doesn't. He's far too lazy. He goes to the nearest place with the right mineral deposits and petrifies the dirt and rocks until he gets the raw material he's looking for. Then he sells the raw material to jewelers, who pay him a fortune for it. Diamonds sell the best, but he hates having to make the trips. Arizona has the best material for diamonds."

"Interesting. Can you turn people into gemstones, too?"

"Typically not."

"But if you did, and you smashed them, would they stay a gemstone?"

"No. Neutralizer would revert them back to flesh, and it's rather unpleasant. All purchasers check stones with neutralizer to make sure gorgons haven't done just that, anyway. Should I be disturbed you're asking?"

My grandmother snorted and waved her hand. "Rufus changed the poor girl's fingernails into opals. After that, I'd be curious, too. She might be thinking we're out to lure her to a secondary location and turn her into an opal for jewelry. Don't worry, dear. Neither one of us would be as dastardly as to petrify someone and turn them into jewelry. If we were going to turn them into jewelry, we'd kill them, strip the flesh from their bones, treat the bones, and use the bones."

I buckled my seatbelt and wondered if I'd gotten my

psychopathic tendencies from my grandparents. "That's good to know."

"I thought so. Since swimming is out, what would you like to do today, dear?"

"What's guaranteed to drive my father insane?"

"Skydiving. He hates planes and believes if gorgons were meant to fly, we'd have wings."

"I've heard that before," I muttered, thinking of the mer half of my family, who also viewed flying as abhorrent. "I'm not sure I'm supposed to be skydiving with a concussion. In fact, I'm pretty sure skydiving is off the list of allowed activities."

"Since when did you ever listen to the doctor's orders?"

I decided my grandmother was the greater threat of the two. "I will be very disappointed if I don't get my lollipop because we went skydiving today."

"You'll survive." She made a thoughtful noise. "Well, maybe. Can never guarantee that when jumping out of a perfectly good plane."

At long last, I had finally found my tribe, and I was blessed to share genetic material with them. I thanked every last deity I could think of before replying, "I'm game if you can convince the old man in the driver's seat."

"We're going skydiving. Now."

My grandfather sighed. "Yes, dear."

ELEVEN

How could you deny me another chance to fly?

THE FIRST CHANCE I GOT, I was going to kidnap my mother and toss her out of an airplane. I'd be generous and leash her to a skilled skydiver first, but I'd treasure the moment I punted her ass out of a perfectly good plane so I could listen to her scream.

I jumped five times before my grandparents convinced me we needed to head home. It had taken all of my grandfather's black mambas hissing to convince me he meant business, and even then, I cast wistful looks at the small plane and its old, cranky pilot.

He thought gorgons stank and made no effort to hide his disgust. After living most of my life around mer, who enjoyed fish, I'd gotten used to odd odors. The musk of a gorgon was hardly a blip on my radar. Hundreds of fish heads rotting on the shores of a rainforest had ensured I had a tolerance for nasty smells.

"One more time?" I begged.

"No," my grandparents chorused.

I returned to my future car, leaned against it, and scowled. "This is cruel and unusual punishment. How could you deny me another chance to fly?"

I'd learned an important truth. I should've been born with wings, and I was happiest the instant I jumped, floating while the wind whipped at me. As soon as I could, I'd learn how to jump alone, taking my fate in my own hands rather than trusting someone else to open the chute so we wouldn't smack into the ground at terminal velocity.

"You've created a monster," my grandfather complained.

"No, I've created positive reinforcement. When she does something we like, we take her for skydiving lessons. She's just like our son. If we want her cooperation, we're going to have to bribe her. Your tally of viable bribes is now up to two. Be grateful."

My grandmother was wise, and I wanted to be like her if I ever grew up.

"I can't win this one, can I?"

"No," my grandmother and I chorused.

My grandfather sighed. "We can't do another dive because it's too late in the day, Tulip. It's too dangerous. While I enjoy a good thrill, I really don't want to have to explain to your father that you died skydiving too close to dark. Thrill seeking is one thing, recklessness is another."

"That's a good reason. Honestly, I need to get back to job searching anyway."

While I'd never admit it, my hand throbbed right along with my head, and skydiving hadn't done me any favors. I'd spend a few minutes making a list of potential jobs to look up, then I'd take the biggest dose of painkillers I could before chasing after sleep.

"And unlike our son, she can be reasonable given a logical

reason. Obviously, Rufus had done *some* research before deciding he needed a mermaid princess as his bride. Now, if only we could convince him to start a hive of his own or have a son. A son would be useful." My grandmother sulked, and her serpents lowered their heads.

They still wore their little hats, and I struggled to contain my laughter at the ridiculousness of so many little snakes wearing tiny hats.

Getting in the car and buckling in bought me enough time to control my mirth, and I grimaced at the twinge of head to toe bruising setting in. By morning, I expected my muscles would be filing a petition to leave the Union right along with my wardrobe.

The skydiving was worth it. I'd regret punching a lycanthrope in the mouth tomorrow around the time the painkillers wore off. After my humiliating defeat by a tiny white pill at the hands of Justin Brandywine, I'd put the prescription painkillers far out of reach, preferably in a trashcan, so I wouldn't be caught off my guard again.

"What do you want for dinner, Tulip?" my grandfather asked.

"Justin and his bacon," I replied.

"I'm afraid Justin and his bacon aren't available for your consumption." Sighing, he got into the car and started the engine. "I'm going to have to warn that poor boy to escape while he can."

"Why would you do something like that?"

My grandmother cackled. "Give it up, dear. Rufus was no different when he first saw his mermaid. Justin's just going to have to fend for himself and ultimately surrender, preferably before she starts taking after her mother and conquering nations to get her hands on him. You should be grateful Rufus didn't attempt to take over the mer kingdom. He would have needed our help, and things would've gotten messy."

I didn't want to imagine a trio of gorgons attempting a hostile takeover of the mer kingdom so my father could catch my mother. Worse, I couldn't guess which side would emerge the victors.

Petrification would give the gorgons an advantage, but fear-induced violence might win the battle.

I'd need a lot of popcorn and a good camera to watch that showdown.

"The object of our discussion isn't making helpful commentary," my grandfather whined.

"Obviously, my father didn't inherit his headstrong tendencies or pride from his father."

My grandmother snickered. "You earned that, dear."

"Perhaps it's better she's not interested in becoming a hive's queen. Kings would wage war to have her, only to learn they'd brought the battle to the hive. Rufus will gain a reputation of producing unobtainable jewels." My grandfather sighed, and unlike earlier, he made a point of obeying most traffic laws. He even avoiding accelerating through the yellows.

"If I don't fall over dead from being some weird hybrid, I'm pretty sure my mother expects me to rule her kingdom when she retires. Not the brightest decision ever made," I admitted. "She'll approve of Justin and his bacon skills, however. More accurately, I think she'll be more interested in his professional responsibilities, as she's certainly not going to find a responsible ruler in *me*."

In reality, she'd been working on me since the day I'd been born, so if I did suffer the unfortunate misfortune of reigning over the mer kingdom as a queen, I had the tools and capabilities of doing the job, the army to support my claim to the throne, and enough islands to ensure I could see to my duties.

If the worst happened and my mother did want to retire, she'd add to her crimes and find some sort of magic enabling me to visit the kingdom I'd be forced to rule. I'd have to step up my bodyguard-avoidance game, as the instant a crown touched my head, I'd have a swarm of concerned mer watching my every move.

My grandfather grunted and turned off the main road for the cobbled lane that would eventually reach my father's home. "Your mother does have a tendency to conquer inhabited islands. When Rufus told me she'd conquered Madagascar, I didn't believe it until I checked the news. I'll have you know, when I was researching her as a match for my son, I had no idea she'd develop such an interesting hobby."

"Hobby? No, it's not a hobby. She takes the conquest of islands very seriously. She's easily bribed, though. A good string of pearls will redirect her attention to another island for a while."

"That seems like a small price to pay for national security."

"I never said it made sense."

"I'm beginning to believe nothing you do does," my grandfather groused.

I smirked, pleased I'd accomplished the one thing guaranteed to keep my more sinister activities off his radar. In a world of murder, mayhem, and vigilante justice, logic ruled.

It was just not logical in the way most wanted to think about, a little like how a mer queen might be dissuaded from conquering islands with a simple gift of pearls. My mother had won the battle with the Queen of England, and the necklace was her trophy.

With one gift, the Queen of England had acknowledged my mother *could* conquer her island, and my mother liked it best when she conquered the places no one thought she could.

It was more fun that way.

MY GRANDPARENTS HAD a fondness for meat, and I thanked my lucky stars they remembered I needed mine cooked. They took theirs raw, and I watched them, brows raised, while they devoured their chicken. The bones occupied them for longer than I found comfortable despite having spent most of my life surrounded by mer, who committed similar culinary atrocities and liked it.

If my father had the same food preferences, I'd be doing Justin a favor if I took him far away.

Long after I'd eaten my fill, my grandparents tore through an entire flock of birds, and I slipped away while their attention was fixated on their meal.

If they asked, I'd tell them the truth. I was tired, my head hurt, and I needed some peace and quiet. I also needed to do some research on my temporary new home. My father would have to live with his disappointment the day I relocated to somewhere new.

My first job would be to identify if Rapid City had a serial killer or two lurking within it. Killers inhabited every city, but serial killers were a special breed, deliberately preying upon others to add to their tally or accomplish their twisted goals.

I fell into the latter category, and my goals involved removing one more threat from society, ideally until no more remained. That would never happen, but with every murder, with every calculated revenge, I came a little closer to creating a safer world for everyone.

Back in my room, I began where I always did, researching the local missing persons databases. The initial count wasn't promising.

Eight men and seven women were labeled as missing, one case was over fifty years old, and the rest had little in common. Most were human, which fell in line with missing persons databases in other parts of America. While magic could give humans an edge in a fight, the other species were a lot tougher. The pair of lion centaurs, missing for five years, intrigued me; lions were an intimidating force, and the brothers had disappeared together.

Their file suggested they'd gone on a hike, never to be seen again.

An unsolved mystery intrigued me. What could make two lions disappear? Why would anyone target lions? Had nature —or magic—caused their disappearance?

The lure of the unknown had dumped me head first into my secret profession right along with my morbid curiosity.

According to the database, the lions had operated a successful business, moving money around to make the already wealthy even wealthier. My interest in investing began and ended with meeting the financial needs of an entire species.

The instant I'd learned how to count, my mother had begun teaching me, taking advantage of my inability to leave land to develop her wealth. One day, she would take over a nation with the powers of her wallet alone, and I dreaded that day.

If she discovered she could assimilate nations through the power of money, her goal would be to rule the entire world. I'd have to stop her, we'd have a fight, she'd probably win and take over the world anyway. Then, angry I'd attempted to defy her, she'd make me manage her new holdings so she could find something else to conquer.

I prayed for good fortune and hoped my father could keep her distracted for more than ten consecutive minutes. With her fear of snakes, my father might even keep her on the run for years before he tired her out and caught her.

Or she hid under the waves where he couldn't go.

With my mother, it could go either way. As long as the chase amused her, she'd keep him nipping at her heels. With some clever encouragements, I could stir up some trouble.

My mother hated losing, and it'd only take a few words to rile her up. Manipulating my father would take more work; I didn't know enough about him to know which buttons to press to get him to do what I wanted.

I'd figure him out soon enough.

I stared at the picture of the brothers, both centaurs smiling for the camera. Before my father had crashed into my life, before my mother had taken over Madagascar, I would've viewed the missing men as my next goal without hesitation.

Finding a serial killer was about solving little mysteries and finding bodies people didn't want found, then from the remains of the dead, piecing together the truth. When I finished with my job of killing the killers, I notified the police so the victims' families could get closure.

One day, my search for justice would lead to my demise.

I'd make a mistake, and when I did, I'd fall prey to someone as my victims had fallen prey to me. The circle would go on. Someone else would eventually take my place, hunting the hunters until they, too, were hunted.

I supposed my interest in Justin stemmed from wanting to one day retire and become an unsolved mystery, unknown by most and soon forgotten by the few. Reality was a brutal thing. When I'd killed my first killer, I'd had no way of knowing how much of a toll death would claim.

Killers like me never retired. Until the day I died, I'd have to keep running and hiding. There was always someone out there who wanted to solve an unsolved mystery.

Serial killers stirred the imagination while stoking fear. Until someone found me, I would be hunted.

Not even a professional bodyguard like Justin could protect me from that, and neither could my mother *or* my father. No one could. Justice came for everyone. I worked to make it happen sooner than later for those who preyed on the weak and innocent.

Above all, I wanted to play at being normal, leading the sort of life good women did when they could ignore the dark shadows of the world. I couldn't. Those shadows ate away at me, too, but I meant to use mine for some good.

It was too late to turn back, but when I didn't allow anticipation to rule, I doubted everything, especially myself. I needed a purpose.

Until I could find something better, solving the mystery of two missing lions would do.

TWELVE

Fishy, fishy, fishy.

EVERYTHING HAD A BEGINNING, and everything had an end. That was the one truth I could rely on. To discover what had happened to the pair of lions, I would need to learn their secrets, which meant research, and a lot of it. The beginning of their end would lead me to their final moments—if they were dead.

Some disappeared because they didn't want to be found, running from something they couldn't face. I'd met a few like that, and when I found them, not the victims I'd believed them to be, I'd turned away and pretended I'd never located them.

Some had been abused.

Some had faced tragedy and emerged broken and beaten but alive.

Some had wanted a better life but believed they couldn't rise from the ashes of their lost hopes and dreams like a phoenix.

Some I had tried to help, leaving them gifts to find. I

checked on those from time to time. Life had many lessons, and one stung more than the others.

Some people didn't want to be helped.

Endless possibilities stretched out before me, and I hoped the challenge would keep me busy for a while. My work began with the names of the two missing centaurs, Luis and Theodore Shaw. As I did with victims of serial killers, I researched the circumstances of their birth; too often for my liking, killers targeted the children of someone they hated, tormenting their true target through the deaths of loved ones.

Either their mother had lied about the identity of their father, or the Shaws were an anomaly; their mother was a human, and their father was an incubus. The incubus likely had enemies; their tendency to cause infidelity among any female with functioning ovaries put them in the line of fire of jealous men.

The women were forgiven for what they couldn't control, but the incubus?

A jealous man would sometimes don the hat of demon hunter and look for some revenge. Human nature never changed, and for those men, it usually ended poorly for them. Where incubi went, succubi surely followed, and they were the next to fall prey to a sex demon on a mission.

How had a human woman given birth to *two* lion centaurs? They weren't twins, either, and they shared the same father.

Fishy, fishy, fishy.

Incubi could reproduce with just about anything, but their offspring usually matched the species of the mother. Magic worked in mysterious ways. I could waste hours trying to figure out how a human mother had carried two lion centaurs to term and learn nothing.

Investigating the mother first would be the easiest; incubi could be thousands of years old, going dormant when magic left the world. In reality, I doubted I'd do more than scratch the surface of the incubus's history. That he'd stuck around long enough to have two children with the same woman interested me.

Why would he stay so long? Two children with the same woman implied *something,* but I wasn't sure what.

Within ten minutes of beginning my search for Alexandria Shaw, I discovered her end. A car accident had claimed her life when her youngest son, Theodore, had been five years old, which led me to a different beginning.

Alexandria was survived by her husband, who happened to be the incubus.

I hadn't known incubi ever married or committed to a single woman. The idea astounded me so much I went to the CDC's online species database.

Sure enough, less than one percent of incubi married. Succubi were more likely to tie the knot with a human man, but the notes claimed such relationships were for breeding purposes only and often ended in divorce as soon as the youngest child reached sexual maturity. Few men managed to ensnare a succubus for life, but it happened, and it almost always involved having a lot of children.

Some things would never cease to amaze me.

With their mother dead long before they'd grown to adulthood, I doubted their disappearance had anything to do with her. It didn't fit.

While disappointed, I did my due diligence, spending several hours profiling Alexandria Shaw, her connections, and possible motivations for someone to target her sons. I saved the file, shut down my laptop, and stared at the darkened screen.

Nothing in what I had read implied Alexandria Shaw was anything other than human, but the existence of her sons claimed otherwise. One lion centaur was a fluke.

Two was a genetic consistency. She hadn't been completely human, but her species remained as much of a mystery as her sons' disappearance.

LIKE MY GRANDPARENTS on my mother's side of the family, my grandparents on my father's side grew bored of me and returned to their home, trusting in the lack of a vehicle to deter me from leaving my father's home. I liked the arrangement; my father kept a few men and women on staff, and when I left them alone, they left me alone.

I had one disagreement with the cook, but we'd come to an understanding within the first twenty-four hours.

He'd let me cook, or I'd twist him into a pretzel. I didn't even need to demonstrate my skills on him, as he sighed, lifted his hands in surrender, and requested I leave his kitchen intact when I was finished with it. As intact gave me a lot of room for error, I figured as long as I cleaned up after myself and didn't destroy any appliances, it counted. And if I *did* destroy something, I'd have the evidence I needed to prove I needed Justin's bacon, else I'd be a risk to myself.

My bacon wasn't anywhere near as good as Justin's, but I turned making breakfast for myself my morning ritual while I spent the first week of my stay at my father's home learning about the area and researching the missing Shaw brothers. I spent a great deal of my time trying to pin down their mother's species, but the circumstances of her birth were as mysterious as their disappearance.

There were no records of her ever attending school.

No hospital had records of her birth, nor was I able to find any evidence she had a birth certificate.

She'd gotten her first driver's license at thirty, a year before Luis's birth. She didn't exist on social media, the internet had little about her, and the one place I'd found where she'd worked hadn't been receptive about my one phone call.

I considered myself fortunate they could confirm Alexandria Shaw had existed and had worked for them for a period of six months.

With more dead ends than leads, a week into my search, I suspected Alexandria truly was the beginning of the Shaw brothers' tragedy, and I had no idea what had led to their end.

Endless possibilities stretched out before me. The brothers could be alive, hiding of their own volition to escape the reality of their heritage. Most men enjoyed being able to claim they were the son of an incubus; such men enjoyed more than their fair share of attention from women until it came time to start a family.

Women wanting a family wanted loyalty, and incubi had trouble in the loyalty department.

Unlike their mother, the Shaw brothers did exist in the system, boasting average talents to go with their species rating. They'd never classify as human, but they had had the next best thing; they were the children of a confirmed human. The law would account for their mixed heritage if they were ever accused of a violent crime.

In the case of wealthy businessmen disappearing, money often led to the killer, so after I built basic profiles of both centaurs, I investigated their business.

It had died with them, liquidated and scattered in the months after their disappearance. One of their business partners had handled the transactions, distributing their workload to several different organizations, all direct competitors. If I wanted to kill someone and get their money, inheriting their profitable business dealings seemed like a good way to go about it.

Lucrative contracts ripe for the picking led many a man to murder.

With motive aplenty, a pair of lion centaurs known for their enjoyment of hunting, and an unforgiving landscape, making them disappear would've been simple. Before I could make sense of the clues and build a digital version of a murder board, I wanted to see where they'd gone and explore the possibilities.

If I could find the scene of the crime, I might be able to find the truth. I smiled.

Others had looked for them, but the others weren't me, and there were many places a snake could go a human couldn't. If evidence of their demise lingered in South Dakota, it was in the national park to the west of Rapid City.

I PLANNED my escape from my father's home at three in the morning, which I loathed, as I'd freeze my ass off until dawn. I'd have to make the first part of the trip on foot, another check mark on my con list. I'd explored my father's home enough to determine he'd deliberately cut off easy methods of escape, and his employees were careful to check their vehicles for stowaways before leaving for the night.

They underestimated my stubbornness.

A normal human could make it twenty miles a day on foot with the right conditioning. Thanks to my inhuman heritage, I could do closer to forty, and I took off at a jog, dodging civilization with my waterproof duffel bag slung over my shoulder. I had expected barren crags and got forests with outcroppings of stone rising between the trees, and the contrast amused me.

I could understand why someone would want to explore one of the few wild places left in the world. Challenging nature had its risks, and the farther I ran from my father's home, the less mysterious the lions' disappearance became. It was easy to get lost in a forest and fall prey to the predators within. The deepest reaches of the national park made an ideal place to hide a body, and I'd done just enough research to understand a million and a quarter acres of protected land made for a difficult search.

When I slithered back to my father's home, I'd have to learn more about the Black Hills National Forest and its secrets.

As woman or snake, I wouldn't let something like the wilderness defeat me.

I stripped, packed my clothing in my bag, and secured it. Then I shifted, resuming my journey across South Dakota to solve a mystery some believed would remain unsolved for all eternity.

For a while, I'd live to prove them wrong.

IN RETROSPECT, slithering across the state wasn't one of my brighter ideas. More prairie dogs than I cared to think about crossed my path, and the little bastards squeaked up a storm when they spotted me. To add insult to injury, many of them were too big for me to comfortably eat.

I made it my mission to find an edible one, and I took sick pleasure in silencing the damned thing. Dragging my prey to the sunniest stone I could find jutting from the dark forest, I swallowed it whole, curled up, and took a nap.

Little beat basking on a sun-warmed rock far from civilization. Lions liked to bask, too, which made it easy to understand why the brothers would seek out the barren stones rising from the forest. A regular human would have trouble climbing them, but I had no doubts a determined lion centaur could reach the top. I could, too, and once I finished sleeping off my meal of delicious, noisy rodent, I began my search for a promising stone column a pair of bored lions might want to climb to escape the world for a while.

I abandoned the first few I found as options; they had foot trails worn into the sides, easy for even children to climb, which made them dangerous but otherwise uninteresting for my purposes. No, if I were a wealthy lion seeking solitude, I wouldn't pick an easy rock. Only the largest one that posed a challenge would do.

Climbing to the top of one gave me an excellent vantage point, as the stones rose over the forest's canopy. Similar rocks littered the park, although one, with jagged, steep sides, looked promising. It was tall enough I couldn't tell if there was space for a pair of lions on its peak, but it was close enough it wouldn't cost me much time checking.

Scouting rarely found me anything concrete, but the

effort gave me a foundation for where to begin searching in earnest. If the rock formations didn't yield anything, I'd look into the deeper, darker places the forest had to offer. It would cost me a few days, but I'd explore the places lions might like to go first, then I'd head back to my father's home, toy with him over my disappearance, and acquire the equipment I'd need to begin the real work of finding lost bodies.

I'd begin with a metal detector, which would help me find coins, watches, or other metal things a pair of lion businessmen might've taken with them on a hike. It would take weeks—maybe months—to search the probable places. If luck abandoned me, it might even take years to find the right bodies. The last time I'd used the method, I'd found six bodies—all the wrong ones—before I'd found who I'd been looking for. Of the serial killers I'd hunted, Randolph Aston had been one of the lazier ones; once he finished with a body, he dug a hole, dumped it in, and left it. He took nothing, he did little to cover his tracks, and the only reason he'd escaped the law for so long was thanks to his talent, which let him dig deep holes in a hurry.

Ten minutes of work, and he had himself a proper grave, six feet deep, ten feet long, three feet wide. Filling it in cost him an extra fifteen, as the bastard had enjoyed covering where he'd disturbed the soil. If he hadn't left metal on the bodies or if I'd used a cheaper metal detector, I never would've found his victims.

A good metal detector made all the difference in the world when it came to hunting bodies in the forest. With the right machine, I could find a zipper at ten feet. If there were people buried in the Black Hills, I'd find them.

Slithering from my perch, I began my search.

WITHOUT CLIMBING EQUIPMENT, a human wouldn't have been able to make it to the top without risking life and limb. Claw marks scarred the stone at the base of the formation, and I didn't want to get into an argument with their owner— or owners. Lycanthropes could tear metal apart, and centaurs were often blessed with inhuman strength, making them the targets of the CDC and law enforcement when anything big, bad, and equipped with swords attached to their fingers caused trouble. Too many options existed for me to confirm or deny what had made the marks.

I only knew one thing for certain: whoever had made them had gone to the top, which meant I'd have to follow for a closer look.

Why hadn't I been born a cat? Or anything other than the daughter of a mermaid queen and a gorgon? Then again, with a saner heritage, I would've led a completely different life. A normal life seemed so nice, so calm.

Instead, I had grandparents who viewed me as a passing interest, a living toy capable of amusing them for five consecutive minutes; even my father's parents had the same tendency, although they'd stuck around for an entire day. I considered it a record.

I wondered how long it would take someone to realize I had given everyone the slip. Hissing my amusement, I slithered up the stones, coiling my tail around rocks jutting from the formation so I wouldn't splatter to the ground far below. I made it to the top to discover a disaster of abandoned equipment, most of it old. Someone had shoved the gear beneath an overhang, and upon closer inspection, I decided a helicopter search wouldn't have revealed the cache, not without flying close to the formation. A pair of lions could bask on the peak, although it'd be a tight squeeze.

Brothers seeking a chance to escape civilization wouldn't mind being crammed together, so I couldn't eliminate the spire as a possibility.

That left me with the tedious job of sorting through the ruined equipment littering the stone. Decaying leather, rusting metal, and scraps of clothes hid a few coins, the newest of which was from five years ago, which matched the disappearance of the two lions. Despite the years, I doubted anyone other than some small animals—and me—had disturbed the remains.

The lack of bones implied the pair, if the pair had left the gear, hadn't died on top of the formation. Had they fallen?

Anything was possible, but it'd be simple enough to burrow a few inches into the leaf-strewn soil in search of bones. I could work in a spiral pattern, nosing through the leaves and dirt, and find surface bones easily enough. If animals had gotten to the bodies, they could be a mile or more from where they'd fallen, although lion centaurs were large enough any predators and scavengers wouldn't have moved them before eating.

If they'd died at the base of the formation, I'd find evidence of their bodies.

If they hadn't, I'd have a mystery layered on top of a mystery, and I'd have to return as a human and gather the remnants to study and test. With my father's meddling, I wouldn't be able to make use of my normal resources. Finding new labs to get test samples from would be difficult, and if I wanted to have any DNA tests done, I'd be stuck with shipping samples to the deep south, making use of contacts that would put me at higher risk of discovery.

The last time I'd used those contacts, I'd drawn more attention than I liked.

Part of me hoped I'd find bones below, but the killer in me wanted a hunt that ended in the death, securing my place as the bigger, badder predator.

THIRTEEN

Mongoose went out of their way to
annoy the hell out of me.

A GOOD SEARCH covered as much ground as possible while also being thorough. Leaving no stone unturned meant I wouldn't have to check over the same territory again unless I needed a metal detector, which I expected I would. Nosing through leaves and loose soil for humanoid remains wasn't my favorite activity, but if someone had died beneath the stone formation, I'd find *something*. Most people wouldn't recognize human remains unless they came across something distinctive, such as a skull or femur.

I'd studied enough to identify human remains, although I wasn't all that good at judging the age of the bones once they'd been stripped of flesh and muscle. When I found bones I needed aged, I sent them to a black market lab for analysis, paying a small fortune for as much information on the deceased as possible. My favorite lab tech had access to CDC databases and could often identify the victim through DNA samples.

Knowing the identity of the victims made it much simpler to find the killer, as every murder had a story.

The trick was learning what bound murdered and murderer together. One day, someone would follow the trail of victims to their killers, and their deaths all told the same story: they died as they had lived, killed as they'd killed. The victims would lead the hunters to the hunter, to me, as I had patterns just like everyone else.

My patterns entangled me with the law, and the law would eventually crack the code, be it through the ties to the CDC entries, the payments to certain labs scattered across the United States and Europe, or the method I used to report the discovery of the bodies, which were always missing a few small bones. One day, someone would put together all the pieces I left in my wake and discover *my* contribution to the story.

Then it'd circle back to the reason why killers like me could never truly retire.

In the meantime, I'd do what I did best, poking my scaly nose where it didn't belong. I found a lot of little bones and evidence of predators dining on the local wildlife before my spiraling search uncovered a pair of underwear, unfortunately used and vile enough I wanted to murder the desecrator of the otherwise nice forest. The sun fell towards the horizon, and as the temperature dropped, I searched for a place to curl up and hide until morning.

I debated between climbing a tree and curling up or burrowing within the rotted remains of a fallen giant; either would meet my needs, out of reach of other predators who might want to try their luck. The only beasts I truly worried about were honey badgers and mongoose; neither were inclined to just fall over and die. I disliked mongoose more than honey badgers.

Mongoose went out of their way to annoy the hell out of me. Between their thick fur and resistance to venom, I classified them as a top threat. Honey badgers were dangerous, too, but mongoose enjoyed their attempts to kill me.

I left honey badgers alone, and they left me alone. I viewed it as an amicable relationship of avoidance. Despite their reputations, I found honey badgers rather reasonable— as long as they weren't pissed off. Once angered, a honey badger stopped at nothing until it acquired revenge, supper, or both.

I liked America; it had a pleasantly low number of annoying predators.

After consideration, I coiled in the branches of a tall tree to wait out the night. If someone bothered me from below, I'd put every inch of my length to good use and teach them why black mambas were to be feared.

THE DAY STARTED COLDER than I liked, and it took me until noon to uncoil from my branch and return to the ground. Moving helped, although my movements remained sluggish. I cursed South Dakota and its weather, regretting my decision to leave the castle designed to keep gorgons toasty warm. The chill turned searching into a slow, miserable affair, although I dutifully nosed through the leaves and debris for any evidence a humanoid had died in the area.

I found nothing.

Night once again encroached on the forest, and instead of climbing a tree, I searched the trunks for a place to hide until the weather turned in my favor. I struck gold among the roots of an ancient giant. Age had killed the mighty tree. Although it still stood, its insides were hollowed so that even a human—or a pair of bored lion centaurs—could fit inside.

Some sentient had discovered the niche, too, carving through the trunk and into the ground. Packed dirt steps spiraled down. A dim glow promised something lurked below.

I considered my options for all of two seconds. The cold mystery I hunted could wait until my curiosity was satisfied. Who—or what—would create a dwelling beneath a long-dead tree? Careful to keep my movements slow and smooth, I descended, tasting the air with my tongue.

Death, in all its stages, had scents and tastes, and the stench of old decay teased my senses. The ground warmed beneath me the farther I ventured, and I basked long enough for the worst of the chill to ease.

The illumination steadily intensified and stained the worked earth with red, creating the illusion blood soaked everything. I nosed at the packed soil to discover it far drier than the moist loam above. The illusion annoyed me into hissing, and I slithered deeper into the ground. Why would anyone build such a place?

I could think of a few reasons, and they all circled to the type of men and women I hunted for sport and justice. If I wanted to terrify someone, I'd begin with a stairwell much like the one I explored. Gouges marred a few steps, and I wondered what had created them. They were deep and long enough to make me believe a large predator had found the space.

The marks reinforced I didn't know enough about the victims I sought; could the marks belong to a lion? Whatever owned the claws could probably cleave bone in half with ease.

No matter what, I couldn't allow the owner of those claws to get a hold of me. I liked being in one piece.

The staircase ended at a tiled landing. More than dirt stained the floor, although I couldn't tell the blood's age. Small bones, shattered by powerful jaws, had been swept out of the way, lining the walls. The bones worried me; sentients tended to sweep the remains of their meals out of the way, not leave them lining a tunnel in a macabre display of lethality.

Some of the larger fragments could've come from a human, which decided me. After I scouted, I'd find some-where to hide for the night, grab a mouthful of fragments, and head for my father's home and send the bones away for analysis. Some species viewed humans and other sentients as prey, and while they didn't classify as serial killers, I'd hunt them all the same.

If the bones belonged to sentients, I'd have my work cut out for me identifying the victims—and killing the killer without joining the collection of remains littering the hallway.

Had I been a little wiser or smarter, I would've turned tail, slithered up the steps, and found somewhere colder but safer to sleep. I'd plan to return as a human so I could collect as many bones as possible before retreating and making plans.

Scouting would give me a better idea of what to expect, as long as the being responsible for the broken bones remained unaware of my presence. My scales rasped on the tiles, and wary the sound would betray me, I waited and listened.

The quiet disturbed me more than anything else; forests weren't supposed to be so eerily still. That mice and the local creepy crawlies avoided the place meant one thing alone: a predator lived nearby.

If I ever did find a way to retire—or found a man willing to put up with me—I needed to make sure I never had a chance to become bored. Boredom got me into so much trouble. Boredom drove me into exploring creepy underground lairs decorated with the shattered bones of some predator's meal.

If I managed to catch Justin, I'd have to warn him about my tendency to create trouble when bored. Nice girlfriends did that, or so I'd been told.

If I tried a little harder to be a nice girlfriend, maybe I wouldn't have trouble keeping a man around longer than a couple of nights. I was my mother's daughter—and my father's daughter, too. No matter how I flipped it, I wasn't a promising prospect to a sane man looking for a stable wife.

If, if, if. There were too many damned ifs in my life, and I needed to change that—if I could.

Damn it.

I'd have to put some serious thought into whether or not a man was worth the hassle of being nice, good, or whatever it was men wanted in women. I suspected a stable career, non-murderous tendencies, and sane hobbies topped the list.

I inched my way forward, and the glow dimmed along with the warmth, tempting me to nest beneath the bones until morning. I endured, restraining myself from hissing my displeasure.

Why couldn't I find a predator with nice accommodations for a change? For some reason, I ended up hunting the sickos who thought an underground lair decorated with bones was actually a good idea.

Ugh.

More importantly, why couldn't I leave well enough alone? I could've turned around when I'd found a staircase spiraling down inside a dead tree trunk, but no. I had to poke my scaly nose where it didn't belong yet again.

I really would get myself killed if I didn't get my head out of my ass and stop testing my luck for no reason other than I could.

A LUNATIC WITH too much money and time had built a maze beneath the forest, and when I found the bastard, I'd put my venom to good use. One bite wouldn't do. No, I'd tap out every last drop of my venom to rid the Earth of the asshole behind the lair.

It wasn't even a good maze; in an effort to disorient, the hallway branched, except the tunnels always circled back to the main corridor, and the idiot with a digging fetish only bothered to decorate the main hall with the remains of its dinner.

To add to my annoyance, the stench of death and decay intensified, leading me to where the predator likely killed and ate its meals—and left them rotting for a while before cleaning the meat and marrow from the broken bones. Most serial killers I'd hunted relocated the bodies once they finished with them. The more depraved kept the bodies long enough for putrefaction to begin, but all of them had eventually removed the bodies.

I'd only killed one man who'd kept trophies, but his

collection had been hair—only hair. It'd made for an easy identification of his victims, leading to closure for the families of his twenty-two victims, all brunette women between the ages of twenty and twenty-five. The hard part had been finding the dumping spot. Of all the killers I'd hunted, he'd been the most creative.

I hadn't been able to save his last victim, but her body had led me to the others, and I'd taken a great deal of satisfaction in his death and sending a lock of his hair to the loved ones of his victims along with a note informing them justice had been served. I'd told their families the stories of their deaths, and I'd left it to each and every one of them on how to get the closure they needed.

Years later, I still felt like I hadn't done enough, that I hadn't found the truth fast enough, that I hadn't acted in time. No matter how many times I'd tried to console myself about my failure, that I couldn't have prevented the last woman's death, I still doubted.

I always doubted.

I'd always arrived a little too late to save their last victim.

I wanted to beat the killer rather than kill between kills, and my failure to do so weighed down on me almost as much as my inability to truly retire.

My long string of failures likely had a lot to do with my flagging desire to keep my true profession the secret it needed to be if I wanted to keep breathing. I liked breathing. If I stopped breathing, I couldn't annoy Justin into running so I could chase him and determine if he wanted to just get away or if he was interested in getting caught.

Once I finished my business in the death cave beneath the Black Hills, I'd do what I should've done in the first place. I'd take a much closer look at Justin and see if I could turn my games into something more. My first job would be to determine Justin's species. It didn't matter what he was; it was the effort I spent learning about him that mattered. Everything mattered, from what he transformed into to his favorite colors, his hobbies, and what he liked to do when he wasn't following my father around.

Once I was certain he'd match with me and I'd match with him, I'd ease him into the truth. He could accept black mamba gorgons. A real black mamba wasn't a far leap. If he could deal with my father, he could deal with me, too.

Worrying about Justin kept me from worrying too much about the denizen responsible for the hellhole I explored. Even if I landed a few good bites, unless I caught the predator off guard, I'd probably be the loser. However oversized I was for a black mamba, no matter how potent, I wasn't immune to harm, nor did I possess a lycanthrope's swift regeneration.

After I transformed, my busted hand would still hurt, and I'd have a new collection of bumps and bruises from my adventures as a snake. I'd probably need a full week to recuperate—assuming I didn't get myself killed being an idiot. I lost track of time slithering down the hall, and when I finally found another stairwell down, I regretted my insistence on exploring the place.

I could've just headed to my father's home, called the police, and let them deal with it. I should've done just that, but no. I'd gotten it into my stupid, scaly head I needed to be the one to determine the truth. I'd seen it before; the police often wouldn't be bothered to check out strange reports until it was far too late to prevent another death.

If there *was* a predator lurking beneath the Black Hills, I needed to know. If I could do something about it, I would.

In a den filled with the stench of death, I held little hope of survivors, but if someone did endure through a living hell, I would do what I could to defy history. I could live with failure as always.

I couldn't live without having tried at all.

And so went the life of a serial killer princess.

FOURTEEN

Great. I'd found another lycanthrope.

WHAT SORT of asshole covered a hole in the step with an illusion and left it for innocent explorers like me to find? Normal humans would've taken a nasty stumble, probably down the steps where they'd break their necks at the bottom. Me? No, I had no such luck.

I fell.

And fell, and fell, and fell until I splashed into nasty, stagnant water. Had I been human, the fall might've killed me, assuming a human could fit through the hole, which one couldn't. Had I landed head first, I would've submerged, drowned, and added to the motley collection of bones. As it was, it hurt like hell, I'd be a living bruise from head to toe, and I'd suffer broken ribs as a human.

In fact, I wouldn't shift back to human until I healed for a while. I liked having intact ribs, and I had no idea how fourteen feet of broken ribs would translate to human anatomy. I expected a lot of pain.

Moving hurt, and it took every scrap of strength to reach the packed dirt beneath the staircase. Larger bones littered the ground, and while the walls glowed with the dim, ruddy light, I hid in the shadows cast by the discarded bones, all of them large enough to be human.

Next time, I'd remember when I slithered around with my head held high, gravity tended to make a mess of things for me, resulting in catastrophe. At least the hole hadn't been wider; bouncing along the edges had slowed my tumble. As far as traps went, I gave the designer credit. In fact, the designer deserved an award for effective trap usage. A few bites would be a suitable reward for good work.

A humanoid would've tripped and possibly snapped an ankle, making them easy—and noisy—prey. I'd thumped my way down and splashed into the water, which had been noisy enough, but as long as I hid among the bones and stayed still, most wouldn't notice my presence. I doubted even a sensitive nose could pick out the musk of a black mamba among the reek of decay. I could barely smell myself, and I knew what I was looking for.

I waited, but no one came to investigate my haphazard descent.

Long after I'd tired of waiting, I emerged from my hiding place and resumed my exploration, my body aching from my nose to the tip of my tail. Like my tumble, no one investigated my vocalized displeasure, and I abandoned my stealthy creep for a more productive search, testing the ground for any more false sections of floor.

I didn't make it far before I discovered another pit with my nose, and I lowered my head inside. For the first few inches, darkness blocked my vision, but once I broke through the magic covering the ground, sound assaulted me. Someone screamed, the high-pitched wail of an ending life, and in the gasped moments of almost quiet, others groaned. A faint glow below betrayed still, dark waters several feet below.

Pulling my head free, I drew my body forward, braced so I could get a better look, and once again lowered my head through the illusion. With a few extra feet to work with, I could make use of the dim illumination to pick out the shadows of the room below.

Bodies hung on the walls, reduced to shadows against dark stone and root-threaded earth. Some lived, the sources of the agonized cries and moans. Most were little more than skeletons held together by scraps of flesh that should've long since crumbled away to dust. I gave my eyes a chance to adjust to the gloom.

Below me, the shallow water hid the corpses of at least two humanoids, so far decayed I couldn't tell their species. A body hung from the nearest wall, close enough I could touch with my nose if I really wanted. I didn't, especially since the poor bastard hadn't been dead for too long; I'd be able to troll missing persons databases for him to begin learning his story—and the stories of the others imprisoned beneath the forest.

I'd hate every minute of it, but his body would allow me to escape the place once I got a better look around—and see if I could save any of the victims. Shuddering at the thought of touching a corpse I hadn't made, I stretched, touched his shoulder, and slithered down his back to the floor. I wish I didn't have to breathe; I could taste the rancid, acrid bite of old death on my tongue. It wouldn't surprise me if in a few days, after I transformed back to human, I'd need to go to the hospital. Diseases ran rampant where death lingered, and I didn't want to think about what was on the ground.

It wasn't dirt, and that's all I needed to know.

I wanted to murder the mastermind for daring to cheapen life so much, creating a hell for those unfortunate enough to still live far below the ground. If I could save even one, I'd accept the risks associated with such a feat. To save one, I'd have to go where I might be found, explain what I'd seen—and how I'd done it.

I'd have to, if I wanted to keep breathing, sacrifice my chance to kill the killer.

Saving one meant more than saving myself. Some problems solved themselves, and no matter what the cost to me, I couldn't let such vile evil walk free to hunt again.

But first, I had to find those who lived and see if any could be saved. If I transformed and risked the broken bones from my tumble, I might be able to get one person out. Otherwise, I'd have to race the clock back to civilization and hope I could return without making the predator aware of my infiltration.

Bracing for the worst, I started counting bodies. Everyone nearby was dead, most of them old enough I'd have to get their identification from bone or hair samples. Three, including the man who'd serve as a ladder for my escape, were fresh enough I'd be able to look for their faces. I did what I could, pressing my nose to theirs seeking any sign of life but finding none.

The first survivor I found didn't have long to live, and she hung by her hands from a hook in the ceiling, her breaths rasping out of her. Human noses couldn't detect encroaching death, but I'd learned its deceptively sweet scent, and when beside her, she stank of it. Old and new bruises mottled her skin, and disease stained her flesh. Pain, too, had a scent, and she reeked of it.

I didn't believe in any faith; I'd given up on the salvation of my soul long ago. I wasn't sure who I prayed to on her behalf, but I did it anyway. I hoped the afterlife had something better and kinder for her, or that she got a chance to live again in a happier world, one that valued her.

Even at my fastest, I wouldn't be able to help her, so I did the only thing left to do, the one thing I'd sworn to myself I would never do. I was no angel, but I brought death to her so she wouldn't suffer through the hours waiting for the inevitable. Picking her throat as my target, I lifted myself up and struck, sinking my fangs in deep.

In a healthy human, it could take hours to die from my bite, although I packed more of a punch than my natural brethren. The lab tests I'd had done on my venom put my potency at unnatural levels, and my minimum dose was over a hundred milligrams per bite more than natural black mambas. With a bite so deep, held as long as I had, she'd gotten a full hit of my venom.

Death wouldn't tarry coming for her, and I doubted she noticed me.

I found four other victims on death's door, their bodies clinging tenaciously to life, broken and waiting to go to the next life. It wasn't until I found the screamer I held hope one might live. He hadn't been hung up to die—he was contained in a cage with the lock out of his reach. I wouldn't need a key; nuts and bolts bound the chains together preventing his escape.

The reason he screamed would be simple enough to resolve. He raged, and his cries promised hell on his captor.

I would help him get his freedom—and revenge—if I could. I saved him for last, checking the others in the prison. Those with no hope of survival I put out of their misery. Two, who might cling to life if I acted fast enough, I left hanging, afraid to move or touch them. I would do what I could.

I slunk to a corner, braced for the pain I'd inevitably put myself through, and shifted. As I'd feared, I'd cracked or broken ribs on my way down, but while it hurt to move, I could, which would have to be good enough. I had a victim to free, an escape to mastermind—and a murder to plan. I'd abandon every last one of my rules when I found the predator behind the torture and death in the prison, giving him the most horrific, painful death I could. I'd take him to death's door, over and over again, nurse him back to life, and repeat until I secured my place in the darkest pit of hell before sending him there first to tell the devil of my deeds.

By the time I finished, the devil would find it a challenge to punish me for my crimes.

I strode to the cage, his scream cut off, and he sucked in a breath. "You're not him."

"I'm not," I agreed, hissing. My torn hand throbbed, but I ignored the pain while I unscrewed the bolt and removed the chains from the cage. I didn't ask how long he'd been a victim; deep underground, there was no way for him to track time, and asking would only hurt more than help. "I found this place by accident."

"Some accident. How'd you get through the maze? He'd let us loose in the maze to watch us die."

"Carefully," I lied, and new worries roused. How could we have experienced such different things? Did he lie?

Was *he* the predator? I tensed, wondering if I'd stepped into a trap of someone exceptionally depraved. If he tried anything, I'd shift, bite him, and be done with him. Maybe I was naked, but I wasn't helpless.

I was never helpless. In time, I'd regain the advantage if I lost it. Lifting my chin, I undid the chains and tossed them away.

"How?" he demanded.

"Luck," I lied again, wondering what would happen when I released him from his cage. "What's your trick?"

"Lycanthrope. I'm a wolf."

Great. I'd found another lycanthrope. "I must be cursed. Aren't lycanthropes supposed to be uncommon? You have the hybrid form?"

He shook his head.

"All right, fluffy."

"Henry."

"Whatever you say, fluffy." I got out of his way and opened the cage's door. "Don't suppose you've seen a pair of lion centaurs, have you?"

He pointed at one of the corners. "I'd say they died a year back, maybe more."

I looked Henry over, who didn't look like he'd been in captivity for a year. "How do you know?"

"He comes down in the morning and likes telling us the date. He keeps me alive because he thinks I'll be useful."

"As *what*?"

"A babysitter."

A maze, an underground lair, bones scattered in the hallways, and a prison mostly occupied by males? I could guess what lurked beneath the Black Hills, and I didn't like it one bit. "You have got to be kidding me. You got grabbed by a minotaur?"

"He's a juvenile," Henry replied, ducking out of his cage and pulling his shirt over his head, which he held out to me. "He's had me here for six years and twenty-three days."

Since wearing a dirty shirt from a living man beat stealing something from a corpse, I pulled the threadbare material over my head. "Lovely. How'd he get a hold of you?"

"I was hiking. He might be a juvenile, but he hits hard." Henry glanced at the woman I'd killed. "She's been here six months. He'd take her to the maze every morning, and she's always refused him. She's the one woman he's caught so far."

"Do I even want to know what he's been feeding you?"

Henry sighed. "Animals. Rabbits, mostly. He'd give me a choice: shift and eat, or starve to death."

I wouldn't blame him for surviving. "And you say he comes in the morning?"

He nodded.

"Time to get moving, then. Follow me," I ordered, heading back to where the hole in the ceiling was. Grimacing over having to touch a corpse, I climbed, used the wall for leverage, and jumped for the ceiling, snatching for the ledge of the hole I knew was there but couldn't see.

Pain lanced up my arms, especially from where I'd punched the leopard in the mouth, but I got my shoulders through the gap and struggled to escape from the prison.

Hands grabbed hold of my ankles, and with a grunt, the lycanthropy shoved me up. "Make space."

I obeyed, scooting away from the opening. Like me, Henry struggled to pull himself through the opening. I grabbed his arm, dug in my heels, and dragged him out of the prison.

The lycanthrope's gaze unfocused, and he stared, his expression turning neutral. "Are you sure you know the way out?"

I decided the minotaur—if it *was* a minotaur—toyed with someone's mind rather than creating an decent physical maze. What I didn't understand was why Henry was affected by it and I wasn't. Then again, it could be anyone with the right talent.

Damn it. Someone capable of rewriting what someone perceived would be a difficult hunt at best. Taking hold of Henry's wrist with my uninjured hand, I limped in the direction of the stairwell.

Everything was as I remembered when I'd tumbled, and having learned from my mistakes, I tested every step on the way up, finding several disguised holes. Henry followed, silent and subdued, obeying my every word without question. It made my work easier, but I worried, too.

How would he react in the so-called maze? I guided him, tensing every passing minute.

At the top of the stairwell, Henry stumbled to a halt, his breaths bursting out of him in short gasps. He twisted around, his gaze darting, as though we stood at an intersection of many halls rather than at the beginning of a straight corridor with an easy run to freedom; the first intersection was at least twenty feet ahead. I tightened my hold on his wrist. "Henry?"

"It's impossible. We'll never get out of here."

I wondered what would happen to him once he reached freedom. Under normal circumstances, my human nose couldn't detect fear or other emotions, but his was so strong it overwhelmed even the pervasive stench of death from below. "Follow me," I ordered, taking a step forward.

"But that's the darkest path."

Whatever magic had been used on Henry, it was strong enough to completely override his reason. Vampires could beguile their victims, but I'd never seen any other magic like theirs. The possibility of a minotaur behind the dungeon, even a juvenile one, worried me. Minotaurs had one use for female sentients: breeding. As far as I knew, males were considered competition or food. Why keep Henry?

Then again, if it *was* a minotaur, a lycanthrope might be able to survive the not-so-tender care of a young minotaur. Stories claimed infant minotaurs teethed on human bones, which explained why there'd be so many imprisoned men.

They were food for future young—or for their captor.

Henry might survive the teething process until he was destined to become the youngling's first meal, something that had likely ensured his survival—for the moment.

I really hoped there was some other nasty behind the lair and not a minotaur. If another sentient viewed me as potential breeding stock, I'd start biting, then I'd beat the bastard to death before my venom could finish the job.

Henry whimpered, but he shuffled along behind me without fighting. At the first actual intersection, he dug in his heels and jerked in my hold. "You're going to run us into a wall!"

"There's no wall," I assured him, dragging him forward. He cried out and fought me. Had he been in his right mind, he would've had the strength to defeat me, but while he struggled against me, I overpowered him and pulled him forward. He yelped before sucking in a breath.

"The wall disappeared!"

"As I said, there's no wall."

"That mother fucking minotaur!" the lycanthrope howled.

I had my doubts the minotaur was real, but I wasn't going to gainsay him without proof. It could be a minotaur. It could be something equally vile, too, playing tricks with his head. It didn't matter; whatever hunted in the Black Hills viewed people as dinner, and I'd been forced to kill out of mercy.

I hoped the man I'd left alive would survive. A better person would've tried to save both men, but with one hand mostly out of commission and my ribs throbbing, I'd have a hard enough time getting Henry out without getting us both killed.

Thanks to whatever was screwing with Henry's head, the lycanthrope would be more of a liability than a help. I found a silver lining, though. Even with him fighting me, it wouldn't take long to escape. I'd moved a hell of a lot slower as a black mamba, checking everything for traps—except the damned stairs.

I really regretted I hadn't checked the steps.

The magic perverting Henry's perception of the hallway strengthened the closer he got to freedom, until he shuddered and closed his eyes, shaking his head.

If I didn't do something, he'd probably run right back to captivity. "Henry, just trust me. Keep your eyes closed. I'll guide you the rest of the way."

The lycanthrope growled but jerked his head in a nod.

With his eyes closed, Henry was a lot easier to manage, although he still flinched every few steps, as though he still perceived something I couldn't. By the time we reached the last staircase so we could crawl out of the damned tree, I shook. Tension, anxiety, and pain conspired against me, but I couldn't stop, not until we returned to civilization.

I wondered if a black mamba could ride a wolf. The thought amused me, and I took a few minutes to catch my breath while regarding the dirt steps with equal measures of trepidation and disgust. "We have to go up more steps, Henry."

"All right," he growled, sounding more like a beast than a man.

Once I got him to the surface, if he showed any sign of shifting, I'd bolt up the nearest tree and hope he'd been telling the truth about only having the wolf form. A hybrid lycanthrope would just rip the tree out by the roots and use it to bludgeon me to death. I'd never met a wolf capable of climbing a tree, so I'd be safe until he lost interest and found something else to hunt.

If push came to shove, I'd spend a few days in a tree as a black mamba, wait until he fell asleep, and go about my business.

Henry kept his eyes closed and stumbled up the twisting, earthen staircase with my help. When we finally reached the top, he shuddered, then he straightened, as though a massive weight had been lifted off his shoulders. Opening his eyes, his gaze locked on the opening, and he scrambled for freedom, a howl bursting from his throat.

The instant he emerged into the moonlight, fur sprouted from his flesh, his bones cracked and twisted, and he shifted from man to beast. He continued to howl, and I shivered at the sound.

I dove out of the trunk's confines, angled for the nearest tree, and grabbed the lowest branch, hauling myself up, jerking my feet out of the reach of the lycanthrope. As I had no idea how far a wolf could jump, I kept going, hissing at the throbbing in my abused, battered hand. My ribs hated me, and the sharp pains made it difficult to breathe.

Given the choice between some torture and a messy death at the jaws of a newly freed lycanthrope drunk on freedom, I'd endure, climb as high as I dared, and play the same game. A human would be an enticing target for a wolf.

A black mamba might not be noticed at all.

With no other choice, I shifted and settled in to wait.

FIFTEEN

Minotaurs weren't supposed to have feathers.

UNLIKE LYCANTHROPES, when I shifted, I didn't ruin my clothes. Henry's shirt tangled in the branches and, despite the abuse, made an ideal place for me to nest. Below, the shreds of Henry's jeans littered the ground, and the wolf bounded in circles, howled his head off, and rolled in the fallen leaves. I assumed he'd gone mad from the joy of freedom, and if he'd been fed nothing but rabbits for years, he'd be hungry enough to eat anything to cross his path.

One day, I'd need to thank my mother and father for their contribution of genes. While accidental, they were the reason I wasn't easy prey for the lycanthrope frolicking below. After years in captivity, I expected he'd start running on instinct, and male lycanthropes had three main objectives: sleeping, eating, and securing a mate.

While lycanthropes interested me, the last thing I needed in my life was trying to be something I wasn't. Henry needed help I couldn't provide. Someone far more patient and nurturing than I would have to ease him back into civilization. Once he calmed—if he calmed—I'd find someone to help him.

Henry rolled to his paws, shook out his coat, and howled. Something was different about the sound, and intrigued, I listened.

Understanding hit me moments later when other wolves answered. With his ears pricking forward, the lycanthrope listened before adding his howl to the chorus, and their song filled the forest. Once they quieted, Henry left, his tail bannered high. Every now and then, a wolf's cry broke the quiet of the forest, and I hoped they guided the lycanthrope somewhere safe beyond his captor's reach.

Whether he'd found a pack of mundane wolves or lycanthropes, it didn't matter. Even weakened, normal wolves were no match for a lycanthrope, and lycanthrope wolves belonged in packs.

They'd welcome him, and they'd care for him. I'd also pay good money to watch a pack of lycanthropes tear Henry's captor to pieces. I'd even deal with the disappointment of a stolen kill for the pleasure of watching.

After I rested, I'd handle the necessities.

I would tell the police of the odd dungeon I'd found underground. I'd warn them of the maze, too, although I had no idea how I'd explain the situation without betraying I'd set a crazed lycanthrope loose in the Black Hills. It occurred to me he was probably a lot saner than I was. I needed to crawl home, hide under my blanket, and reevaluate my choices while trying to make sense of the hot mess my life had become.

Had I been in my right mind, I would've focused my attention on the killer of my serial killer. Loose ends could get me killed, and until I found out who had killed him and why, Matthew Henders's story wasn't over—and mine could come to an end if the killer had connected me to my would-be victim somehow. It was possible.

To isolate Henders as the serial killer, I'd tested hundreds of samples, inquired with numerous missing persons databases in the northern United States, and even pretended to be a victim's friend. I was tired of the life I led, and that led to mistakes. I'd flitted from interest to interest, looking for *something* to make life worth living.

That Justin Brandywine and his bacon topped my list should've been warning enough I'd begun self-destructing. Too many changes in my life didn't help, although when I thought about it, my life was nothing but one change after another.

I didn't know what it was like to have a house I could call a home like my father did. I didn't understand what it was like to have my loyalties bound to a kingdom like my mother did. I had goals, but they shifted from day to day, murder to murder. I'd considered the idea of retiring, but the truth had always prevented me from turning my desire into an obtainable dream.

My story was one of isolation and loneliness, of a solitary predator in search of purpose, wrapping horrific deeds in the thin veneer of justice. In that, I'd done well enough. I'd found justice for many. I'd found peace for many others, and I'd given it to them as a gift, offering the closure the police couldn't—or wouldn't. I was never sure which. If I, working alone, could find the truth, why couldn't the police?

I was determined and dedicated, but I wasn't special. Anyone could do as I'd done—and I suspected some could do it better. Hell, many could do it better. Most would've been satisfied with finding the truth and allowing the legal system to do the rest.

I'd strayed by taking matters into my own hands and spilling more blood. Imprisonment never seemed enough, not for the criminals I hunted. Only death could secure safety for potential victims. I'd told myself that until I believed it.

And I did. People like me couldn't just step back and reform. We were, to our very cores, killers. I chose to kill those who deserved to be killed. Others chose to become predators for the thrill of the hunt and to satisfy demented desires. No matter how I boiled it down, we were all the same breed of bird. I just dyed my feathers a slightly different color so I could pretend I was better than my brethren.

Everything circled back to the same realization: I was tired.

Before I returned to civilization, I needed to rest and recover from my descent into the hell lurking beneath the Black Hills. While I waited, I'd watch. After sunrise, I'd return to civilization and hope the lone survivor trapped below would hold on long enough to be saved.

A MONSTER PROWLED through the forest below, and at first glance, I could understand why someone would believe it was a minotaur. It was huge, easily ten to twelve feet tall, had the head of a bull with horns sharpened to lethal tips, and sported massive cloven hooves, which sank into the forest floor. Then, a whisper of wind blew through the forest, and its tracks disappeared, the scattered leaves rustling while the soil reshaped itself to mask the presence of the beast.

Minotaurs weren't supposed to have feathers, nor were they supposed to have tentacles. The monster beneath me had four tentacles sprouting out of his shoulders, and they swayed in the air, the suction cups gleaming with slimy fluid. The pervasive stench of death clung to it, a match for the horrors of its den.

Maybe it had started its life as a minotaur, but whatever it was, it wasn't just a minotaur anymore. I kept still and quiet, watching from my hiding place within Henry's shirt.

The hooked claws on its long-fingered hands would make short work out of me—and my tree—if it discovered my presence. I expected to die, but I didn't want it to be at the hands or jaws of a monstrosity. Worse, I understood Henry's reaction to freedom.

I would've gone mad from joy if I'd escaped the horror beneath me, too. Had I counted my captivity in years, I doubted I would've made it half as far as Henry had before becoming overwhelmed. I'd hope the monster's magics couldn't reach Henry beyond his lair. Guilt, apprehension, and self-preservation waged a brief but fierce battle. If I left, I'd save myself from the risk of becoming its prey, too.

If I left, Henry might become a victim again. If I left, I might be able to save the survivor within.

I'd have to hope my venom could down a beast like the one stomping around the trunk of his tree, snorting and huffing, lowering his head to breathe in the mixed scents.

I bet the damned thing smelled me, a female, near his territory, as he snuffled and searched, going down on all fours to nose through the leaves near the opening. Then it found the scraps of Henry's jeans and bellowed its fury.

If the minowhatsit found Henry's shirt, he'd find me, so I abandoned my impromptu nest and slithered higher into the tree, wrapping around the trunk and a branch, hoping to blend in with the bark and avoid notice. Being noticed wasn't a part of any of my plans, and I didn't want to know how a fight between us would work out.

I expected to join the bones lining the damned thing's lair, although if things worked well, he'd join me in the grave. Unless I got exceptionally lucky, I wouldn't emerge unscathed—if I emerged alive at all. Nope, I had zero intentions of fighting a mutant minotaur.

Maybe I was crazy, but I wasn't completely off my rocker yet.

At least I could verify Henry hadn't been off his rocker, either, although I had no idea how I'd avoided the minotaur's influence. I'd heard the myths, legends, and rumors about them. My first step into the minotaur's lair should've been my last as a free woman, easy prey for him to capture me at his leisure.

And since I, just like the poor woman I'd killed in its lair, refused to become breeding stock for some damned minotaur, I'd come too close to death for my comfort. Not only had I come close to death and captivity, I wouldn't have died doing something useful or paying the consequences for my version of vigilante justice.

The minotaur bellowed again, slashing at Henry's torn jeans, leaving deep grooves in the soil. His magic once again whispered on the wind, undoing the damage he caused. I hated that part of his foul magic almost as much as his ability to create mazes and toy with his victims' minds. Without evidence a large predator lurked within the forest, I understood how so many had fallen prey to him. Too many relied on trails and other signs to keep safe, especially centaurs and lycanthropes.

Vanilla humans wouldn't know the difference between a man-eating minotaur and a goat unless slapped in the face with one. Then again, no one expected a minotaur, especially not a mutant one.

The minotaur continued to bellow, pausing only to snort and suck in great breaths. Pawing the ground with a hoof, he lowered his head and charged one of the neighboring trees. His head collided with the trunk, which exploded in a shower of splinters and bark, and the entire thing toppled with a ground-shaking boom.

Yep, if I let that damned thing get a hold of me, I'd be pulverized. All I could do was sit tight, wait, and hope he didn't take offense to my tree. While the wind blew and the minotaur's magic whispered in the air, not even it could hide the evidence of his fury, leaving behind the fallen tree as testament to his preternatural strength.

I needed a new life, stat.

THE SUN ROSE, but the minotaur remained, stomping around the entrance to his lair, slashing at the remains of Henry's jeans, and snorting, punctuating his displeasure with the occasional bellow. I wanted to hiss at him for his persistence, but I remained still and silent.

Three trees had fallen prey to his temper, and he was running out of targets before he'd inevitably smash my tree into mulch. I'd become a black mamba pancake.

There were better ways to die, and I spent an unhealthy amount of time considering them in turn. Choking on an ice cream cone topped the list, with tripping over my own feet and falling into traffic, a paper airplane to the eye, and a thousand infected paper cuts making a good showing. I'd rather choke to death on my own spit, too.

Something rustled in the underbrush, and the minotaur whirled around, stomping a hoof, and slashing at the air.

A flash of yellow drew my eye, and a large form, almost a match for the minotaur, burst out from the bushes. Its high-pitched scream startled me into hissing. With one look, I recognized the newcomer. When stuck between a rock, a hard place, a minotaur, and an overgrown yellow mongoose with a death wish, it was time to get the hell out of Dodge and pray to the devil the two combatants didn't notice me.

I was done with the Black Hills, and I swore I'd never return, not even under threat of death. I could handle waiting for a minotaur to lose interest.

If I stuck around, the mongoose would climb into my tree, scent me out, and eat me. It'd do so head first, and it'd enjoy every last nibble of delicious snake treat. It'd leave a few scales behind when it finished with me as a promise to other black mambas it had no fear of us. It probably thought my venom was tasty.

Uncoiling from the trunk, I made my descent, using bark and branch as launching points to reach the ground. The instant I landed, I darted away, keeping my head low and hightailing it out of the area, obscuring my passage by lurking beneath as many leaves as possible. If either noticed me, I didn't want to see them catching up; while I could move fast, I couldn't move monster fast.

I had no hope of winning a race against either a minotaur or a mongoose.

Being eaten alive took top spot on my list of things I

never wanted to experience, with someone snatching me by the back of my head and plucking me off the ground as a close second. I hissed, thrashing in the futile effort to free myself. The grip tightened, not hard enough to hurt, but ensuring I couldn't escape without help.

Why couldn't mambas be constrictors? A constrictor would've viewed my predicament as a challenge to overcome. My captor lifted me up and turned me.

If I never came nose to nose with my father's black mambas ever again, I'd be happy. They hissed at me, and my father's scowl promised some form of new hell for me to enjoy in the near future.

I hissed back, lashing my tail. Since being held behind the back of my head wasn't comfortable, I coiled my body around his arm to alleviate some of the pressure.

"We're going to have a very long talk about this," my father promised.

Unable to bite and wary of becoming a living but petrified piece of jewelry for his amusement, I limited my protests to unhappy hisses.

My father sighed before whistling.

Normal people had dogs who heeled on demand. My father had an overgrown yellow mongoose, who bounded over, crouched at my father's feet, and licked blood off its muzzle. Infuriated my father would dare consort with a natural predator of black mamba kind, I hissed my displeasure.

The minotaur followed, and it'd taken the brunt of the fight, lacerations covering its head and muzzle, with no evidence it'd gotten a hold of the mongoose. It lumbered forward.

My father straightened and every last one of his serpents reared back. Then he hissed.

The minotaur opened its mouth, took a single step forward, and a gray film rippled over its fur, accompanied by the crackle of fragmenting stone. Seconds stretched into minutes, and while the initial paralysis had been almost instantaneous, the minotaur labored to breathe while its body stiffened, darkened to gray, and petrified into stone.

Kneeling, my father held out his hand, his grip firm on the back of my neck. "Hold her," he ordered.

The yellow mongoose made a soft, purring sound before capturing hold of me with a paw, gripping me as my father had. I hissed over the rival predator's enjoyment of my captivity.

I hadn't even known mongoose could purr.

When I saw a mongoose, I left the area before it noticed I was around. It probably enjoyed gloating over having played a part of my capture after having beaten the snot out of a mutant minotaur. In its shoes, I would've been feeling quite pleased with myself, so I couldn't really blame it.

My father circled the minotaur his serpents hissing at the impotent statue. "What is this thing?"

I flicked my tongue to taste the air and got a mouthful of death, decay, blood, and fury, none of which appealed when I was within a single snap of a mongoose's jaws of becoming a memory. While I doubted my father would deliberately let his pet mongoose eat me, I wasn't going to bet on it.

I was a bad enough daughter that threats of breeding a replacement made a great deal of sense to me.

"I think it started life as a minotaur," the mongoose growled.

Great. My living nightmare could talk, which put it—no,

him—in the shapeshifter or lycanthrope category. He talked, he purred, and he had enough strength to pop my head right off if he wanted, assuming he didn't decide to enjoy me as a morning snack.

"And he smelled my daughter in the area," my father hissed.

Balling his hand into a fist, my father took two steps towards the petrified minotaur, jumped, and lashed out. While my father's hand looked like flesh, he treated the minotaur's head like the minotaur had treated the trees, resulting in a powdered mess of stone.

My mongoose captor chuckled, a deep, rumbling sound. "Lesson learned."

My father shook out his fist, strolled to us, and reclaimed me from the mongoose, and the pair worked together to wrap every last inch of my fourteen feet around his forearm. "Thank you, Justin."

Of course. I shouldn't have been surprised. What other type of species would be capable of working with a black mamba gorgon with any hope of surviving a bite? My luck was truly the worst. If I wanted Justin and his bacon for life, I'd have to sleep with the enemy, who could eat me the instant I stepped out of line.

I was truly my mother's daughter.

I drew lines on that job.

PRIDE DEMANDED I ESCAPE—OR at least struggle. My time spent up a tree hadn't done me any good, and neither had becoming a piece of living jewelry for my father's amusement. I ached, and even when my father tested his luck and released his hold on the back of my head, I was too tired to bite him.

Even my fangs hurt, something I'd never experienced before.

Leaving the beheaded mutant minotaur, my father marched through the forest with Justin bouncing alongside him. I wondered how many times I could bite the lycanthrope before my venom would do anything other than annoy him.

Thinking about him made it easier to ignore the bumps, bruises, and broken bones. I'd never considered a mongoose as a partner before.

They could eat black mambas, which went at the top of the con list. However, they could eat black mambas other than me, which went at the top of the pro list. If I bit him, he wouldn't fall over dead, which gave him an advantage over other potential lovers. Not killing my partner took spot two on the pro list, although losing my most potent self-defense weapon took spot two on the con list.

The only option was to make Justin Brandywine suffer for a lifetime for daring to be a mongoose. Every morning, I'd begin with making him make me bacon. Some goals in life I couldn't sacrifice, and good bacon was one of them.

He'd obviously, somehow, determined my nature—likely my father's fault—and had begun his clever schemes to infiltrate his way into my affections using my one true weakness. Once I shifted back to human, I'd have to have a long discussion with my father. Was he unaware mongoose ate black mambas? Did he lack fear because of his gorgon heritage?

I bet it was because he was a gorgon. Obviously, my father cowed other black mambas by parading his pet mongoose around. As I had a severe objection to *my* prey—a mongoose!—being someone else's pet, I'd have to take steps to take him from my father and make a proper arrangement with Justin. A mongoose was a good predator.

While I couldn't retire, I *could* obtain a partner in crime. Having a partner would help me restore my past, careful practices. It wouldn't be just me taking a fall. I'd thought about it—I'd even already considered Justin as a potential.

A mongoose lycanthrope with the hybrid form had to be at least as rare as the bacon he made. The problem was, what was I supposed to do with a mongoose? I didn't want him heeling like some pet, obeying my every word.

I wanted a challenge. I wanted to be the predator as much as he was the predator, equals in our lethality.

My first challenge would be rescuing him from my

father's clutches. My second challenge would be teaching my father he would never, ever make *my* mongoose heel like some dog. I'd have to spend a great deal of time coming up with a suitable punishment. I'd involve my mother in some fashion, assuming I could get her to stay in the same room with the gorgon for more than five minutes.

I still questioned how I'd been born in the first place. I also didn't want to think about if I was the result of an inter-species quickie.

The possibility annoyed a few hisses out of me, and I eyed my father's wrist. One bite probably wouldn't kill him, would it?

"Don't even think about it," my father warned.

I raised my head, opened my mouth, and displayed my fangs in warning.

"Tulip!"

I hissed again, beating his arm with the tip of my tail.

"I left you alone for one week. Then you decided to run away and become the prey of a minotaur. You are in no position to hiss at me, young lady. What were you thinking?"

"With all due respect, sir, it *is* possible he lured her out here. Why else would she come out here? There's nothing here." Justin bounded forward a few strides, stretched out, and shook himself, tufts of yellow fur shedding out of his coat. "I'd consider it fortuitous she had enough control of her faculties to climb a tree and stay there. It's also fortuitous he was too stupid to climb up after her."

"Or he had no idea she was there and smelled a female he couldn't find," my father grumbled. "To try to touch *my* daughter. When you get to the car, take her home. See if you can get her to shift back to human. I'll return to his lair and evaluate the situation."

"I'll call the police as well."

"Yes, do. They're welcome to what's left of his body for study."

"I'm sure the CDC will be pleased to be given a gift of a beheaded minotaur."

I hissed my approval of Justin's sarcasm and began the tedious process of untangling my coils, reaching towards the ground. Before I made it far, my father grabbed the back of my head. "Where do you think you're going?"

Justin rose to his full height, seized the back of my head, and used his other hand to gather my full length. "I'll save you the walk back to the car. Should she refuse to shift, I'm sure I can stuff her into a bag for transport."

"Justin," my father warned while his snakes hissed their displeasure.

With a low, rumbling laugh, the mongoose wrapped me around his arm, kept hold of the back of my neck, and bounded off, his run consisting of long jumps. The way he moved suggested he was accustomed to carrying something in his left hand while in his hybrid form. My first thought was a gun, but I discarded the idea; why would a lycanthrope need—or want—a firearm?

The minotaur could pulverize trees with his head, but lycanthropes with the hybrid form could rip cars apart without putting much effort into it.

I'd have to make sure Justin understood there'd be no destruction of any vehicles I wanted to claim as my own.

Capturing a lycanthrope, obviously, would only be the beginning of my problems. Caring for one and taming him enough he wouldn't destroy me and everything I wanted to own, would be a challenge. I'd also have a lot of work to do in the untaming department. I'd have to do something about my father to ensure Justin wasn't controlled.

Under no circumstances could I allow *my* future partner in crime to heel to anyone, not even me.

ALMOST EVERY PROBLEM in life could be solved with a nap, or so I liked to believe. Justin won a great number of points recognizing when I went from alert to dozing. When he arrived at a dark sedan parked at the edge of the forest, he opened the driver's door, snatched clothes from the passenger seat, and set me down. Then he started the engine, cranked the heat, and left me alone.

He shifted, revealing a deceptively lean, soft body. I suspected his muscles hid beneath his skin, waiting to be flexed. With no sign of fear, he took hold of me behind the head, transferred me to the passenger seat, and dressed before sliding behind the wheel. "I see no reason to force you to shift," he announced, reaching over to open the glove box. He retrieved a cell phone, and he dialed a number. "I've made it to the car, sir. She's mostly asleep, so I'm going to let her be. I'll crank the heat in her room, settle her in, and stand guard in case he's part of a herd."

I liked that his tone allowed no argument, and I also liked he hung up before my father could say a word. I didn't like the idea the mutant minotaur from hell, recently relieved of his head, might not be a solitary entity.

Justin drove, and I rearranged myself on the seat, coiling properly so I could bask in the hot air blowing on me without agitating my collection of bumps, bruises, and probable broken bones.

I couldn't remember most of the ride, and I stirred when he transformed my bed into an oversized nest, placing me in its heart. True to his word, he cranked the heat high enough I was comfortable; I suspected Justin sweltered, and his solution to the problem was to strip and shift, hopping up on my bed as a mongoose, the kind I didn't want to battle in the wild.

I watched him, kept my fangs to myself so I wouldn't provoke him, and waited.

At my lack of aggression, he jumped into my nest with me, rammed his nose under my coils, and shunted me aside.

I uncoiled and moved to reclaim my territory.

With what I interpreted to be a mongoose grin, one that displayed his snake-eating teeth, he swatted my nose with his paw, then he bounced, swaying in place.

I hated mongoose. I hated the smug little bastards. Since biting—and potentially killing—my future partner in crime wouldn't work, I'd have to come up with some other tactic to browbeat him into submission. I reared up to my full height and hissed at him.

Justin dared to purr at me.

Since killing him wasn't an option, I'd teach him that there were ways I could use all fourteen feet of my length to put him in a bind. Humiliation wasn't lethal, and I'd enjoy when my father discovered I'd used my natural weapons in unexpected ways to keep my opponent tied up and unable to bite my head off for annoying him.

I couldn't help myself. I enjoyed a challenged.

JUSTIN CHEATED. I had no other explanation for how we'd ended up a tangled mess, rather than me binding him with my coils and remaining in full control of the situation. Sometime during bringing all fourteen feet of my length into play and wrapping around my furry nemesis, I'd become knotted in several places.

I'd done exactly what I'd set out to do, trapping the squirming mongoose. Like me, he avoided using his natural weapons, claws and teeth included, which was likely how we'd become a living pretzel, so twisted we'd need an intervention to escape the situation.

I still counted it as my victory. My goal had been to ensure he couldn't escape. As I'd accomplished my goal, I'd be content.

I yawned, wiggled enough I could burrow my nose into his warm fur, and took a nap.

A bark of laughter woke me, and I displayed my fangs for the intruder, lifting my head with a long, low hiss. Not much had changed since I'd decided consciousness wasn't a requirement; Justin remained tangled in my coils, although he'd squirmed to make himself as comfortable as he could.

My father leaned over my bed, and his serpents canted their heads to the side as though at a loss.

"Please tell me you know how to shift, Tulip."

I flicked the air with my tongue, and as he had asked a reasonable question in a pleasant tone, I bobbed my head.

"Is there a reason you haven't shifted?"

I nodded, then I pointed my nose at Justin, who remained asleep despite my father making enough noise to wake the dead.

"I fail to understand how Justin is responsible for your current status as a rather lovely black mamba, if I do say so myself. I should've guessed you were your own supplier. Do we need to have a long talk about the appropriate use of your fangs?"

Annoyed over his incorrect belief he could control how I used my fangs, I hissed and burrowed my nose back in Justin's fur where it belonged.

"And here I thought you'd be more like your mother. She made it halfway across the planet before she realized I wasn't going to hurt her." My father gently took hold of the back of my head, peeling me away from Justin, trailing a finger along my back. Making a thoughtful noise, he released me, pinched Justin by the scruff of his neck, and lifted us both up.

When alarmed, mongoose barked, and Justin thrashed before blinking and realizing my father held us hostage. Both of his ears twisted back, and he showed off his snake-eating teeth.

My father rolled his eyes at Justin's display. "Unless you want to stay tied up with a black mamba rope all day, settle down. And to think my parents want me to have an entire hive of children tormenting me until I die of old age. I have enough trouble with one daughter. To make it worse, unless you get your act together, I'm going to be stuck with both of you. You just had to introduce her to your cooking skills, didn't you? Taking advantage to my family's weakness to bacon was low, even for you."

Justin lifted and turned his head with a satisfied huff.

Grunting his disapproval, my father resumed untangling us, and I found it amusing neither one of us made any efforts to help him. When I was finally freed, I returned to my nest, coiled up, and hissed.

"You need to shift back to human," my father replied, still holding Justin by the scruff of his neck.

I reared up, opened my mouth, and showed off my fangs.

"Don't you get mouthy with me, young lady."

While I counted as young to him, there was nothing lady-like about me, so I darted forward and snapped at his hand. He yelped, jerked back, and dropped my future partner-in-crime. Justin bounced on the bed, rolled, and bounded across the comforter. I flicked my tongue and pursued, slithering along the edge to keep him from escaping.

"Seriously? Play with him later, *after* you tell me what you think you were doing, Tulip."

I swiveled my head to hiss at my father, which was when Justin pounced, grabbing hold with his front paws and driving me down to the bedding. I lashed my tail and waited.

Checking his watch, my father sighed, shook his head, and strode to the door. "Fine. I'll be back in a few hours. Try to be human by the time I return. We're going to have a very long talk."

I wondered if all parents believed such threats were effective. My father left, closing the door behind him and leaving me alone with the number one natural predator of black mambas.

AS HAVING HANDS WAS USEFUL, I slithered off the bed and headed for the bathroom so I could shift in the tub and soak away the aches and pains. It hurt like hell, and through the entire process, I had a curious mongoose voyeur keeping me company.

"You're a pervert," I rasped, and as I was too tired to make a fuss over it, I didn't bother to try to hide the mottling of bruises covering me head to toe. "Lycanthropes suck. You just shift back and forth a few times, and you don't have to pay the bill for your idiocy. Me? Oh, no. I'm going to be a bloody mess for weeks."

Shifting *had* helped, although I wasn't going to admit it. My tentative exploration of my ribs indicated I'd gone from probable breaks to bone bruises, which were far superior to fractures. It would hurt, but unless I started coughing up blood, I wouldn't go to the hospital.

Lycanthropes cheated. Justin shifted quicker than I did, and he did so with fluid grace, growing and melding with his human form until he knelt beside the tub, his arms draped over the side. "This explains so much," he murmured, looking me over while I went about filling the tub and adding shampoo to the water so I could have bubbles.

"Being a freak of nature does explain a lot of things," I conceded.

"I was trying to figure out how a reptile lycanthrope could exist; lycanthropes are exclusively mammals. From our observations, we'd determined you'd inherited cold-blooded traits from both sides of the family, but we were beginning to believe you were a vanilla human."

Me? Vanilla? I snorted and splashed the water. "The CDC refuses to believe I'm immune to lycanthropy, and since I don't have another trick I'm willing to prove, I look vanilla. I'm sure they'll give me an immunity rating one of these days."

"Or you can register as a shapeshifter."

"That'd be rather stupid of me."

"Would that be because you have a tendency to find your way directly into trouble that might require you to use your fangs to eliminate threats?" Justin rested his chin on his forearm, watching me with a smirk. "I've been studying you, Tulip."

The way he purred the word studying made me want to think he had a few ideas for a more thorough examination of my person. "I thought you couldn't stand the sight of me."

"As a rather skilled predator, one of my first tricks to lure another predator out is to act like prey. I ran and, because you're a predator as I suspected, you locked on and hunted for me. Had I known you weren't cut from your mother's cloth, I would've lured you off somewhere in private and begun my campaign to win you sooner."

I narrowed my eyes. "Why? Because let's face it, that sounds about as creepy as me wanting you for your bacon."

"I've been watching you for a long time," he admitted with a shrug. "Part of my job. Your father's interests are my interests. As his interests involve making certain you, his only living child, remain safe, I've been keeping an eye on your activities. You're a magnet for trouble. Were you aware that you almost fell prey to a sexual predator?"

I cocked a brow, and I considered how I'd discovered Matthew Henders's body. A hybrid mongoose lycanthrope could've easily done the damage with a single claw, and it fell in line with how they liked to kill, going for the throat and killing the snake by the head. "Were you aware my mail was going to explode?"

"No," he growled. "I've learned you have a serious problem with mail bombs."

I scowled, twitching at the thought Justin might've been the one to yank my prey right out from beneath my nose. "You were the one to kill him, weren't you?"

"I had reason to believe you were his next target."

With my cheek still twitching, I wiggled my toes in the

water. To my dismay, they ached, too. "Yes, that was the entire point."

He gaped at me. "What?"

Rolling my eyes, I fashioned my hand to resemble a gun and mimed shooting someone. "Let's say there's someone I really don't like, and I have a really good reason to dislike them. Well, I have this bad habit of killing them, especially when they're someone like Matthew Henders. He was an irredeemable ass of the worst sort. I got onto that mail route specifically so he'd notice me." I heaved a sigh. "There's just no artistry in a slit throat. Really. Couldn't you have at least used some finesse? I had everything planned right to the second. Except the mail bomb. That was *not* a part of my plan."

"You were planning *what*? To become his victim?"

I leveled my worst glare at him. "No, you idiot mongoose. I was planning to kill him. Also, he wasn't a sexual predator. He was a serial killer with rapist tendencies. There's a difference."

Justin blinked. "He was a serial killer with rapist tendencies?"

"I do believe I just said that."

"You knew he was a serial killer with rapist tendencies, and you went near him anyway?"

I flicked bubbles at him. "That is the idea. How else was I going to kill him?"

Slumping over the edge of the bathtub, Justin bowed his head and groaned. "This is even worse than I thought. Next, you're going to tell me you went after a minotaur on your own on purpose."

"No. I was actually looking into the disappearances of two lion centaurs in the area, poked my nose where it didn't belong, and found his lair. I found the centaurs, but they're dead. At least I don't have to try to explain away that one. He had a lot of victims. I mercy killed some of them, but one inside might survive if someone gets to them sooner than later. There was a wolf lycanthrope I guided out, but he went loco the instant he got through the maze. That's actually why I was up the tree; I didn't want a crazed lycanthrope getting a hold of me." Lifting my hand, I showed off where I'd punched the cat in the mouth. "Last lycanthrope I tangoed with got punched in the mouth for trying to wreck my future car."

"We heard. That's why your father's back here rather than trying to convince your mother she should come home with him again. It wasn't going well."

"Well, yeah. Snakes eat fish. Was he *really* expecting a different result?"

Justin snorted without lifting his head. "And mongoose eat black mambas, yet here we are. We're both in the same bathroom. No one's dead yet."

"I'm a woman with simple needs, Mr. Brandywine. I already told you. I fully intend to have you make me bacon every morning for the rest of my life."

"You realize that's not exactly a good reason to dedicate to someone, right?"

I wrinkled my nose, lifted my chin, and turned my head so I wouldn't have to look at him. "If you're looking for sane, you're barking up the wrong tree, mongoose. Maybe I just like bacon that much."

"Or you have no social skills, have no idea how to have a relationship with anyone, so you're willing to work with what you understand, which happens to be bacon." Laughing, he lifted his head, reached out, and flicked bubbles in my direction. "And you prefer lycanthropes because you understand once you land a lycanthrope, you don't have to have relationship skills; he'll make it work because the virus ensures it."

As I couldn't deny his accusation, I shrugged. "So what?"

"Are you actually monogamous?"

"I've tried relationships. The bastards kept looking at other women, so I left before I resorted to murder."

"You haven't actually murdered any of them, have you?"

"I don't date my prey. That's just rude."

"You just strut so they notice you, then?"

"Well, how else am I going to get close enough to kill them?"

Justin grimaced. "How many bodies have you left hidden around? Dare I ask?"

"Why would I hide the bodies?" I asked.

He jerked his head up, his eyes wide. "What do you do with them, then?"

"Report them anonymously so that the police can bury the fuckers. I don't leave messes to be cleaned up. I kill my victims properly, thank you. And unless they have habits of leaving *their* victims on their door step, I don't leave their bodies just lying around anywhere. No, Mr. Brandywine, I very deliberately leave my bodies to be found, along with a very detailed explanation on why I killed them." Frustration over having been thwarted by a *mongoose* welled up, and I wailed, "It's not fair! You slit his throat and just left him there. How could you? That's so sloppy."

"And here I was worried your erratic behavior was due to the shock of seeing a corpse."

"No, it was due to the shock of some sloppy jerk stealing *my* kill and just leaving him on the step for anyone to find. I had it planned to the minute. You hear me? I had it planned to the *minute.*"

"You're not going to accept any excuses, are you?"

"There is no excuse for a sloppy murder. You're going to have to do better than that."

"You have no problems with me killing, you just have a problem if I don't do so with the proper grace?"

"That sounds about right, yes."

"There's a word for people like you, Tulip."

"Insane? Psychotic? Sociopathic? I have an entire dictionary of words that match my base tendencies. All of them come from a psychiatric health dictionary for some reason."

"I was more thinking along the lines of incredible, but those might fit, too. So, you have jealous tendencies and the desire to murder any man you're with who strays. How do you reward undying loyalty?"

"I'm not into dead people."

Justin groaned, hung his head, and then laughed. "Neither am I."

"That's good. I can work with a mutual disinterest in necrophilia. I killed a necrophiliac once. I drew lines on that job. I beat him with a stick rather than violating him, because that's just damned gross. Actually, I stuck to standard physical violence and made do when I killed the real sickos. It was a challenge sometimes. Still, I made them all suffer the hells they put their victims through."

"I'm strangely relieved you have limits."

"I have rather strong urges to bite men I want to keep around permanently. I haven't bitten anyone yet, mainly because I'd kill them. That really puts a damper on potential relationships. I don't want to be a black widow. I'm a black mamba. What's the point in having a man if he's just going to fall over dead on me?"

"Two things. First, I'm a yellow mongoose. I can—and have—eaten black mambas for breakfast. Second, I was initially hired because your father could bite me without needing a new bodyguard. I've learned black mambas have an inherent need to bite someone when they're pissy. Really, my job mostly involves being available if your father needs to bite without killing someone. I tend to protect others from your father instead of the other way around."

"I'm considering recruiting you as my partner. As such, you'll never heel at my father's command ever again. Should he try to make you heel, after I'm done beating him to death, I'm going to make sure you've learned your lesson. I have no problems with you continuing your efforts to keep him alive. For some reason, I almost like him."

"I'm sure his contributions to your life have something to do with that. Otherwise, he's somewhat annoying."

"He is. And his parents? They're almost as bad as my mother's parents. Now, that said, I'll tolerate them if they take me to jump out of perfectly good planes some more. I liked that."

"Anything else I should know?"

"I probably won't have a long lifespan. That, plus I'm technically a serial killer. I just happen to prefer killing other serial killers. So, one of these days, I'm probably going to be tossed in prison or executed."

"Just how many people have you killed?"

"This year?"

Justin closed his eyes, slumped beside the tub, and sighed. "Sure, let's start with this year."

"If you hadn't so rudely taken my kill, I would have had

two serial killers in the bag. I bit a few people in the minotaur's prison. They were dying, and I wasn't sure they could be saved even at a good hospital. They were too far gone."

Cracking open an eye, the lycanthrope watched me. "How'd you know?"

I tapped my nose. "Death has a scent, and it clung to them. They were in really bad shape. I left one alive hoping he might be saved."

"Excuse me," he murmured, rising and striding out of the bathroom. A few moments later, I heard him speaking to my father and telling him there might be a survivor in the minotaur's lair. He hesitated, and then confessed I'd bitten several victims as mercy killings. When he returned, he was still naked and didn't have his phone with him. "He'll take care of it. If it can be verified it's a mercy killing, it won't be much of an issue. At worst, he'll pay a fine to the survivor's family and swear under oath they were put out of their misery and couldn't be saved."

"I could make that oath."

Justin crouched beside the tub. "He'll be happier if he deals with it. He's a typical gorgon. The idea his daughter is self-reliant won't settle well. Females in gorgon society are treated like prized jewels to be protected and treasured by the leader of their hive."

"I absolutely refuse to share my man," I hissed.

"I find this very promising."

I scooted in the tub to make space, although it'd be a tight fit if he decided to join me. "I don't share men, but I'm willing to share my bath. You seem to have misplaced your clothes. You have to be cold. The water's warm."

"I should be reminding you I'm a lycanthrope, which makes your suggestion a rather dangerous one."

"I'm pretty sure we already determined I have no social skills, and I've already come to terms with the reality I'm never going to be a good girlfriend or whatever it is I'd be."

"As I'm a lycanthrope, you'd have to accept the title of wife. I don't mind accounting for your relationship handicaps, although I'll have a few rules."

"What rules?"

"No escaping allowed. Once you're mine, you're mine. I will hunt you should you try to run. I'll even enjoy it."

"No heeling at my father's command. That's not allowed."

"You realize that was a hunting strategy, right? If I'm at his feet in a crouch and he uses his gaze, I won't be affected by it. When he whistled, he indicated he was ready to petrify our opponent. I lured the minotaur into your father's range. I wasn't heeling."

"You heeled like a well-trained dog. Never again."

"What should I do, then?"

"Bite him."

"You're being unreasonable about this."

"No, I'm not. There will be no heeling. You can go stand behind him looking smug, but none of this crouched at his heels like a good dog. I'm unwilling to negotiate on this point."

Justin rose, dipped a toe into the tub, and joined me. I expected him to slide in, which he did. However, he did so in such a way I sprawled over him, and his chuckles rumbled in his chest. "I accept your terms. If you're going to insist on hunting serial killers, I'm going to insist you do so through legal channels."

I jerked, sitting up so I could stare at him with wide eyes. "There's a way to kill them legally?"

He sighed. "Yes. It requires licensing with the CDC and

certain law enforcement organizations, but yes. There are ways. You really didn't know?"

"What I was doing had been working until you came along and stole my kill!"

"I'll help you get legalized, and I'll even help you with the hunt, but you're going to have to walk me through all your past kills so I know what I need to do to protect you."

"Aren't you supposed to be my father's bodyguard?"

"If he fires me, he fires me. I'm a lycanthrope. The instant I take you to my bed, you'll be my top priority for the rest of our lives, and all other loyalties come second. I'm sure there'll be an excessive amount of whining from certain individuals."

"I have this tendency to wander off. You probably want some nice, reliable woman."

"I'd get bored," he murmured, wrapping his arms around me. "I'm also willing to put up with the heat cranked up so you won't get cold."

"And my bacon?"

"Most mornings, I'll make you bacon. I've learned it's best to come armed with food to keep cranky snakes happy in the morning. Bacon is a common weakness among gorgons, and I've learned to take advantage of it. I think I'll be enjoying my morning bacon duties a great deal more in the near future."

"Does it have to be your bed? Because really, right now, that's a deal breaker. I'm going to have a hard enough time getting back to mine."

"I'm not worried. For now, enjoy your bath, and I'll take care of the rest."

NOTHING LATELY WORKED TO PLAN, not that I had much of a plan. Aware of my bruises, Justin held me in the tub, and he was so warm I was content to stretch out on top of him and doze while the water soothed my aches and pains.

"Did you break anything?" Justin asked, sliding his hands along my arms.

"Shouldn't you have asked that earlier?" I shrugged, grimacing at the pull of strained muscles. "I shifted enough times that if I cracked anything, it'll hold."

"I should have, but I didn't realize how bruised you were. You seemed energetic. After, we were too busy wrestling to worry about it. I'll know better in the future. You have no sense of self-preservation."

"Lately, I haven't," I agreed. "I'm usually a lot more careful. I'm just tired. I'm tired of running, hiding, and waiting to be hunted down, too."

"Well, there's no reason you can't rest, relax, and regroup for a while. Once you've had a chance to heal, we can evaluate the situation. I'll definitely need to research your kills and find out how hard it'll be to hide them—or create enough evidence to legalize your targets. I expect this'll cost your father a great deal of money. It'll make him feel better about himself, especially when he realizes you're as much of a predator as him and your mother. Gorgon females are vicious, but only when they're threatened. That's a trait of the males, and males are rare."

"My father is an endangered species?"

"Essentially. From what I can tell, he wants to begin rebuilding his hive with your mother as his harem queen. He was hoping to begin gathering new females by making an arrangement with another hive, trading the matured daughters of a hive. In exchange, you'd become a gorgon prince's surrogate, his harem queen. Your father'll have to make another plan, as I'm going to claim you for myself despite his wishes."

"You tricked me," I accused. "You ran so I'd chase you."

"And I hoped you were as weak against bacon as your father. In case you were wondering, you're even worse."

"I also have a weakness for lollipops."

"Only the ones with pixie dust in them."

"Well, yes. Why else would I want a lollipop?"

"I can probably make sure you get a lollipop now and then if you're good."

A better woman wouldn't have fallen so easily to bribes. "How am I supposed to be good?"

"You'll let me carry you to bed, get you tucked in, and I'll call in a doctor to make certain you're all right. Then I'm going to join you in bed and mark my territory until there's no doubt you're mine."

"I have this tendency to want to bite," I warned him.

"I'm sure I can handle whatever you throw at me. If you like to bite, bite. You're not going to hurt me. Even if you do, I'll heal. I'm just worried I'll hurt you."

I hissed. "I'm not a fragile little flower."

"No, you're not. You didn't even need us to come to your rescue, did you?"

"The minotaur would've gotten bored and wandered off eventually—or I would've dropped on his stupid head and bitten him so many times he frothed at the mouth. Either way, I would've won. You just made my escape easier."

"And you really weren't lured there?"

"No. I told you, I was bored. I decided to see if I could solve a mystery. I just did a sweep of the forest and nosed around as a snake until I found the minotaur's lair. I found a bunch of camping gear on top of one of those stone pillars, so I figured there was a body in the area. I'd been searching for bones. If I found any, I was going to send them to a lab for identification, then I'd handle it depending on what I found. That's usually how I find a serial killer; I find the victims first, learn what I can about them, then go after their killer."

"How long can you go before you get bored?"

I laughed and shrugged. "Not long. Sorry."

"It's a good thing I appreciate a challenge. It wouldn't do for either one of us to get bored."

To be continued...

Thanks for reading!

The next novel in the Magical Romantic Comedy (with a body count) series is Whatever for Hire. These stories can, with the exception of Burn, Baby, Burn (sequel to Playing with Fire,) be read in any order.

Afterword

Unlike other Magical Romantic Comedies (with a body count,) Serial Killer Princess is only the beginning.

There will be other tales of Tulip and Justin told. Serial Killer Princess 2 will be fun, and I look forward to going on a brand new adventure with this crazy couple with you.

As of December 2020, Serial Killer Princess 2 is slated to be included in an anthology of Magical Romantic Comedy short stories, novellas, and short novels.

Date TBD.

~RJ

About R.J. Blain

RJ Blain suffers from a Moleskine journal obsession, a pen fixation, and a terrible tendency to pun without warning.

When she isn't playing pretend, she likes to think she's a cartographer and a sumi-e painter.

In her spare time, she daydreams about being a spy. Should that fail, her contingency plan involves tying her best of enemies to spinning wheels and quoting James Bond villains until she is satisfied.

RJ also writes as Susan Copperfield, Bernadette Franklin, Audrey Greene, G.P. Robbins, and Lilith Daniels. Visit RJ and her pets (the Management) at thesneakykittycritic.com.

Follow RJ & her alter egos on Bookbub:
RJ Blain
Susan Copperfield
Bernadette Franklin
G.P. Robbins

Audrey Greene

Lilith Daniels